DOMINOS

DOMINOS

A Novel

Donna Calhoun

iUniverse, Inc.
New York Lincoln Shanghai

Dominos

iUniverse books may be ordered through booksellers or by contacting:

iUniverse
2021 Pine Lake Road, Suite 100
Lincoln, NE 68512
www.iuniverse.com
1-800-Authors (1-800-288-4677)

Because of the dynamic nature of the Internet, any Web addresses or links contained in this book may have changed since publication and may no longer be valid.

This is a work of fiction. All of the characters, names, incidents, organizations, and dialogue in this novel are either the products of the author's imagination or are used fictitiously.

ISBN: 978-0-595-44776-3 (pbk)
ISBN: 978-0-595-68969-9 (cloth)
ISBN: 978-0-595-89094-1 (ebk)

Printed in the United States of America

CHAPTER 1

▼

I stood over the body, looking down on the remains of this man, thinking that it should not have been this easy. It was too easy to kill another human being. I had done it; I had killed this man. I'd been killing for years, but not like this. I was not a killer of people. My killing experience had been with deer hunting, duck hunting, that kind of thing. Animals, not people. When you hunt deer, one minute you are sitting with the deer in the gun sight, the deer is alive and well, peaceful. The next minute, the deer is on the ground, its blood flowing out onto the cold, red Alabama clay. It's hours of boredom and five minutes of adrenaline rush.

I know when I am deer hunting that when I make the kill, I have to wait long enough to know that it is down for good before I get out of the hunting house and walk over to the body. I usually wait fifteen to twenty minutes; waiting gives the animal enough time to bleed out. This keeps the animal from getting up and running again if it sees you before it has sufficient blood loss to leave it unconscious. After twenty minutes, you get out of your tree and walk over to the prey. With the barrel of the gun, you lightly touch its open eyeball to make sure it's dead. I learned from years of experience that if the prey was not really dead, he would not lay still for a gun barrel to touch his open eye.

I had hunted for more than thirty years in the woods of south Alabama. In a bad season, I would kill one deer, but in a good season, as many as four. I killed my first deer when I was fourteen years old—old enough by south Alabama standards to hunt. Southern kids generally learn to hunt when they are big enough to hold a gun steady. When I first started hunting, I had no idea that killing this man would be more satisfying for me than killing any deer, and that I would feel no more remorse for killing him than killing any animal. I had actually felt worse killing a deer because they were beautiful animals; this guy had added zero value to the human race. I thought killing a man would have been harder in some way, but as it turns out, I was wrong.

I didn't even need to plan, really; it all seemed to fall into place. This was just like any other hunting trip: watching the prey come into my sight, waiting for it to turn just a little to the right to face me. I remembered to slow my breathing and to hold the gun steady but firm. Then I moved the sight up to his face for a double check on his identification, although I knew it was him. Who else would it be here in his own backyard? Two of the first rules of hunting are to know your prey and what is in front of and behind your prey. Overshooting a target can be a very messy situation.

I lowered the gun sight back down to his heart, or in this case, where his heart should have been. I could not believe this monster had a heart. For a deer, you try to hit the heart by taking a shot just behind the shoulder blade to line up on the heart. A heart in this guy was questionable, but I knew that whatever engine drove this man was in there somewhere, and I needed make that engine stop. I checked my breathing as I always did before I pulled the trigger. One deep breath, hold it a second, and let it out slowly while carefully squeezing the trigger with your whole hand slowly to keep from jerking the gun. I had repeated this motion innumerable times; I had practiced shooting that very gun for years. I was very comfortable with that gun, target practicing with it many times. I knew you shouldn't jerk the trigger, that moves your focus off the target and the end of the gun just enough to make you miss.

I did everything that I knew I should have done as a hunter. I squeezed smoothly through the shot, holding the gun snug against my cheek and keeping my open eye on the target until the very end. I watched the prey drop like a buck in the late season as the bullet of the .308 passed clean through his chest. The impact was visible before the sound registered in my ears. A .308 was my deer gun of choice because it left a good-sized hole at the exit wound, and I didn't need to worry about the prey running far, if at all. As I found out, it also dropped a human male pretty easily, too. The man dropped to his knees, then straight down to his chest. I noticed a large red stain on the back of his shirt. My initial response was to pump my fist in the air, but I didn't. I was actually surprised that the body didn't fly backwards like it does in movies, but he just dropped more like a crumple than anything else, falling down like something had taken the bones out of the body.

My rule with deer hunting was to wait to approach the carcass until the deer bled out. This kill, of course, was different; waiting was not an option. Though I knew that nobody was around for several acres, the sound of a .308 carried, and heaven knew who could have heard the shot. After I watched the prey fall, I sighted the man on the ground through the scope just to make sure that he was not getting up or moving. I looked down and found the spent shell casing next to my foot. I did not want to leave behind any evidence that might indicate the type of gun I used. I knew that the police would be able to match the gun type eventually, but there was no reason to help them by leaving the casing behind. I had enough experience in hunting to know that you never leave the shell casing behind; it told other hunters that you have been there, but it was also just plain sloppy to leave casings behind in the woods.

Slowly and in complete control, I got out of the stand and walked over to the body. I looked down and saw that his eyes were still open, just like a deer's would be laying dead on the ground. I put the gun barrel to his open eye and touched it very lightly. Because I had hunted for game and eat what I harvest as a rule, this was a new experience for me. I had never killed for pleasure and I wondered, though briefly, if this kill was for pleasure or if it was my duty. I didn't shoot varmints or birds just for fun. I'd been raised to understand that you eat what you shoot. Not this time, however. This time I turned slowly and walked away from the body, leaving the remains to rot in place. Good riddance to bad rubbish.

I walked back through the thick, musky woods under the shadows of early dusk. I was temporarily confused by where I was going because it was so much darker than it had been on my previous scouting trips here, which were all earlier in the day than dusk. I could barely see my feet, so I slowed my pace to keep from falling as I crossed over the muddy bottom of Polecat Creek. All I heard was the sound of crickets, a sweet and peaceful sound of a summer night in south Alabama. I had spent some time in these woods, but not nearly as many hours as I had at the hunting camp.

It was always a good idea to watch your step walking in the woods here this time of year. There were tons of trip hazards, and snakes were always a concern during the warm months. The weather got warm and the foliage got thick, so the creatures were happy to curl up around a log, and you didn't know they were there until you either stepped on them or were close enough for them to strike. It would have been just my luck to kill a guy and then have the police find my body in the woods, dead from a snake bite.

As I walked through the brush with quick, controlled steps, I listened to the sound of my own breathing. It was deep and steadier than I would have dreamed it would be. I had more control than I thought I was capable of in that situation. The moon gave me just enough light through the trees to get back to my truck, only four hundred yards away from the fresh kill. I did not look back, but I did listen to make sure that I did not hear anyone coming. I did not think about my physical condition until I sat in the truck and took off my muddy boots. My hands were shaking and I had started sweating. I had a slight headache—the kind you get when you read all day without glasses if you need them, the kind of headache that did not go away with an aspirin.

It was buck fever. I laughed at myself because I'd never been known to suffer from buck fever. But it sure felt like I had a major case of it now. The control I had just moments ago was fading fast; I needed to get out of there. Buck fever was caused by the adrenaline rush you got from looking at prey in a scope and waiting to pull the trigger. Often, there was no time between seeing the prey, pulling up the gun, making sure that you had a good shot, and pulling the trigger before you got buck fever. It could be minutes or seconds before you got the fever. Most hunters suffered from some form of buck fever, but I'd been lucky and never had it—until this time. I've had the post-kill adrenaline rush in previous hunting experiences, but this was different. My heart was racing, my hands were sweaty, and I had no recollection of the last thirty minutes. I knew what I had done but could not seem to remember the details. I remembered I was in the stand and then, in an instant, I was back in my truck. Did I really do what I thought I had done?

The thought hit me. This kill was, without a doubt, the biggest "buck" I had ever tracked and killed. This seemed absolutely hilarious. I wondered how many Boone and Crockett points I could get if I reported this kill. Boone and Crockett points were an assessment standard for calculating the quality of an animal based on several physical characteristics. I saw a picture in my mind: my kill hanging by its feet on the hook at the weight station, me standing beside the body for a picture. In my fantasy, my gun was in my right hand, and my left hand was holding the kill by its matted, dirty hair so the camera got his mud-streaked face. I saw me smiling for the camera, then framing the picture later for my vanity wall in my office at home.

The night was getting darker, but as the clouds overhead cleared, I saw the moon. What a beautiful night. There were no house lights anywhere around, and I could see the stars shining brightly in the sky. I realized that I was surely going into shock from the events of the last couple of days, but I was powerless to do anything about it now.

I started laughing again, harder this time, and I had to try more than once to remember how to start the truck. It took two tries before I got the key in the ignition and one more try before the engine turned over. I had been driving these roads for years because I had grown up not far from here, so I slowly pulled out of the red clay road and onto Highway 55, heading north toward home as if on remote control.

I laughed until I pulled into my driveway ten minutes later and hit the garage door opener. As the garage door opened, I looked at myself in the rearview mirror and saw that even with the laughter, there were tears rolling down both cheeks. Isn't that strange?

CHAPTER 2

▼

"Cold toes are the worst things in life," thought Katie Race as she wiggled her size-four feet in her borrowed size-seven hunting boots. "My toes are freezing."

It was opening day of hunting season: November 20, 1976. Young Katie sat fifteen feet above the cold hard ground in a leaning metal tree stand. Tree stands were ladders with a seat at the top strategically attached to trees by hunters and placed in the middle of deer crossings. Deer cross from their sleeping places to their eating places in the morning and back to their sleeping places in the late afternoon or evening. This metal hunting stand was a little noisy. Katie had noticed when she got into it that morning that if she didn't sit very still, it squeaked slightly. Katie knew that this would scare the deer away and she reminded herself again to sit very still.

White-tailed deer only do three things: sleep, eat and mate. A white-tail deer's life is a simple life, a good life, until the Saturday before Thanksgiving when the woods filled with hunters. Hunting season in Alabama and other places in the country was a very big event. Diehard hunters plan for this day all year. Hunters look forward to opening day like small children look forward to Christmas morning.

Today was not only opening day of hunting season, but it was also the first time that fourteen-year-old Katie had been allowed to sit in a tree stand by herself and possibly shoot her first deer. Katie had been hunting with her dad, Byron, for the past four years and this year, Katie's mom allowed the persistent girl to attend the hunter safety training and get her own hunting license. Katie had started whining non-stop last season when her friend Billy Greene, one year older than Katie, had gotten to hunt by himself. Katie complained that if he could hunt by himself then so could she. The constant needling by Katie and her dad started on the last day of the previous hunting season, January 31, 1976. It continued all summer until they had gotten on her mom's last nerve, and she had agreed that if Katie would hunt close to her dad, and Katie would agree to take the hunter safety class, *and* she would get good grades for the whole first semester of school, then and only then, Katie would be allowed to hunt by herself. Katie had done her part: met all the minimum requirements for hunter safety, gotten okay grades, and practiced her shooting at the firing range before opening weekend.

Though Katie knew her dad loved taking her hunting, she understood that the biggest reason he agreed to let her get her own license and hunt on her own was because having a fidgety teenager in the hunting house was a major pain in the ass. Hunting houses at Perdido River Hunting Club were built out of plywood and placed on stilts between ten and twenty feet in the air. Though there were a rare few hunting houses built for two people, most were constructed to house one hunter at a time. With Katie and her dad in the same hunting house, it was crowded, so the houses they could both fit into were limited. This restricted where her dad could hunt. Byron had suffered this inconvenience for years because he knew his daughter loved to hunt. But he also knew that his freedom was in sight now that she was getting bigger. After all, the best part of hunting was being alone.

The other problem with having a teenager in the hunting house was that she couldn't sit still. The plywood did little to muffle sounds coming from inside; every move was amplified through the woods. Katie had spent endless hours with her dad sitting as still as a child who is bored and cold could, and honestly, she did better than most kids her age. The floors, ceiling and walls of the houses were made of plywood, without much else. The smallest foot slide by Katie across the plywood floor sounded like a drum banging in the middle of a deserted football field. When constructing a hunting house, builders tried to keep them quiet by putting worn carpet remnants on the floors. When Byron helped with the construction of these houses, he always talked about Katie's inability to sit still when constructing the houses. The carpet on the floor helped a little, but it didn't conceal all the sounds in the graveyard silent woods. The point, after all, was to surprise your prey and making a great deal of noise didn't help with the surprise element.

A hunting house was like a phone booth a little larger than normal but not as tall. Katie thought that being trapped in a hunting house felt like being trapped in a cardboard box with air holes cut in the sides. The house was generally no more than four feet by four feet, with a wooden bench that numbs a person's butt after sitting on it for five hours straight. It generally had small windows, six inches high by thirty-six inches wide on all four sides, which gave the hunter a panoramic view of the woods or the clear-cut they were watching. Katie and her dad had perfected the scouting by assigning each window to one or the other. When it was hot, Katie and her dad baked. When it was cold, they froze. The houses always seemed to have some crawly thing in them: wasp, bees, rats, lizards or flying squirrels. But Katie had learned to deal with all of this, because she loved the excitement of hunting and the time she got to spend in the woods with her dad.

Byron belonged to a Hunting Club in the north end of the county for years before he starting taking his kids hunting. Perdido River Hunting Club had been in existence since 1961 when a small group of friends got together and approached International Paper Company about leasing land to them to hunt. The deal was made to benefit everyone concerned, over barbecue at Mama Lou's and a great deal of cold beer. International Paper had worked many of these deals to lease land to hunters all over the country, and south Alabama was no exception to the rule. The original lease agreement stated that the twenty male members agreed to pay one dollar per acre for the privilege of hunting for white-tail deer, pigs and turkeys. All of the original members lived close by the property and this kept them near their families during the weekends of November, December and January.

At that time, Bay Minette, which was the closest town to the hunting property, was a much smaller town than it was in 1976. Most of the original members of the club were local law enforcement or attorneys who had limited time to travel to north or central Alabama where the deer were bigger and the hunting better.

The lease agreement worked well for the International Paper Company because the primary reason for owning the land was to harvest for pulpwood. Harvesting required that the trees, mostly pine, be clear cut periodically, then the company replanted more baby pine saplings, let them grow, and the process began again. The benefit to having the property hunted was the less "damn deer" they had to deal with, the better. The paper companies did not appreciate the "damn deer" eating the baby trees they attempted to grow, so less deer, less loss of trees.

From a conservation standpoint, south Alabama had very few natural predators for the deer population, and the control of these herds in the 1960s and 1970s was a problem. The deer population rose dramatically and traffic accidents from deer running out into the road in populated areas were on the rise. The other, even sadder, consequence was that the natural food supply couldn't keep up. With the population growth, the deer were getting smaller and smaller. Deer were traditionally small in this area of the country since there was no need for them to have a great deal of winter fat because of the warm weather. Now that their numbers had grown, they were starving to death due to overpopulation. Even the environmentalists and tree huggers of the '60s agreed that something had to be done to minimize the effect that these deer had on mankind and on the overall health of the deer. Katie had been raised to understand that the responsibility that went with hunting including understanding the consequences of hunting on the animals. She had also been raised understanding that not everyone approved or understood the effects of hunting on the population.

Hunting in the south had always been a way of life but hunting increased in popularity as a recreational sport during the 1970s. Perdido River and International Paper struck their deal to support the growth in the sport. IP was smart enough to put their land under the Alabama Conservation Land Management program, which required that all hunting clubs meet certain minimum requirements. The hunting clubs were required to track the population of the deer on their leased property by documenting the harvest. In practical terms, this meant that all harvested deer had to have certain measurements of horns, points, size on bucks and on does, if they were showing signs of milk. Additionally, all game management program participants had to extract the jaw bones from all their deer and turn these over the game biologist who would "age" the deer to track the overall population of the herd. Katie was well aware of the rules and regulations of hunting in that area.

Alabama was known for huge amounts of deer, even though they weren't large, and the racks were smaller than in other parts of the country. The white-tailed deer in Alabama drew hunters because of their volume and taste. Because the deer fed on natural vegetation, the meat was healthy and cheap for enterprising rednecks. Alabama was also known for its long hunting season and good weather from November to January. The hunting season was seventy-five days long, which was three times the length of most states' seasons.

Byron Race had started hunting at Perdido River in 1965 when Katie was just four years old. Byron worked for the county as the Human Resource Manager and later, as the County Administrator. He'd been invited out to the hunting camp by Mark Crabtree, a founding member of the club. Mark, who had hunted since he was a child, was constantly recruiting new members into the sport and into the club.

When Byron had been 'recruited', the two of them had been sitting at the Elks Club with several other guys from the hunting club when the subject turned to

Byron having never hunted before. Mark, who was Byron's best friend, had joked over several shots of Jack Daniels that night, that Byron was a wimp because he was not a hunter. Byron made his thoughts known to everyone at the bar that it did not take a huge amount of talent or intelligence to sit in a cold box, wait for Bambi's mother to walk into a planted food plot, and blow her away with a high-power rifle with a scope. This was very funny to the nonhunters in the room but not for the hunters who took the sport every seriously. The five other guys sitting at the bar, all hunters, stared for several minutes at Byron before striking back. If he thought it was so easy, he could get his ass up to the hunting camp next Saturday, and they would be glad to explain the fine art of hunting the great white-tailed deer to him.

Byron agreed to join them, leaving his confused wife, snickering from the door at four o'clock in the morning, to drive the twenty minutes to the hunting club. Byron didn't own a gun and had no intention of hunting with anything other than a camera. Photography was a recently acquired hobby, and he thought it a good time to get some practice. On the first outing, after they placed him in a stand, he got comfortable in the chair and immediately fell back to sleep. When he woke up an hour and a half later, there were five deer standing in the food plot just twenty-five yards in front of him. He slowly picked up the camera and began snapping pictures.

Before the hunt that morning the hunters had agreed to stay in their houses for five hours. After the designated time, a pickup truck came bumping down the sandy dirt road with three of Byron's buddies in the cab. As they pulled to a stop, Bryon walked over from where he was sitting on the side of the road with his camera.

"What did you see?" Mark said, laughing, the answer from his smart-ass friend should have been "not a damn thing" because that was what Mark and the other two had seen themselves that morning.

"Five," muttered Byron as he cleared the dust that the truck had kicked up out of his eyes with his sleeve. "I saw five."

"Five what?" scoffed Duck Gunney, opening his first beer of the day at 9:00 a.m.

"Five deer, ya dumb shit. Isn't that what we've been out here for five hours waiting on?" Byron bit back as he climb into the back of the truck, putting his camera safely in his lap.

"Five of what kind of deer?" pressed Harold Shurfeld, "You non-hunting, non-gun-owning newcomer. You think we believe you were the only guy that saw a deer this morning.

"The fuzzy brown kind of deer, Harold. What do you mean, what kind of deer?" Byron asked, closing the door behind him.

"Did you see a boy deer? They have horns on their heads. Or a girl deer? They don't have horns on their heads," asked Mark, now laughing so hard that tears were rolling down his cheeks.

"Boy or girl deer? Kiss my ass. I know the difference," yelled Byron. "There were two bucks and three does. Why, what did you guys see?"

Everyone stopped laughing, and the ride back to the camp got very quiet. It took a great deal of time to get all the answers out of Byron, but basically just to keep the guys quiet, he decided that a camera was a waste of time, and that on the next hunt that afternoon, he would take a borrowed gun. Byron shot his first deer that day, an eight pointer, meaning that it had eight horns on his head. Many of the regular members passed it off as beginner's luck, but Bryon couldn't pass up the chance to say that it had nothing to do with luck; it was just that easy to shoot deer. Which is the same thing, he reminded them, that he had been saying while sitting in the warm, smoky bar at the Elks Lodge with a cold beer in his hand. There was nothing to it. But something bigger happened that day, what happened that day was that Byron learned he loved to hunt, and years later he passed this love on to his only daughter at a very young age.

Katie loved her time with her dad, the two of them alone in the hunting house. When Katie was very small and first starting going with her dad, he had taken crayons and coloring books to keep Katie quite. Katie tried so hard to be still and quiet. She often fell asleep, lying in the floor of the hunting house while her dad stared out at the open field. The more time she spent in the house with her dad, the more she learned about the art and science of hunting.

Now, this was Katie's big day, her first hunt without anyone watching over her. While Katie sat freezing in the ladder stand, she thought about all the deer she had seen while hunting with her dad for so many years. She told herself again that he was a lucky hunter. He saw more deer than most of the other members of the club, and he had recommended that she sit here on number sixteen for her first solo hunt. This was a hunter's favorite time of day, when the sun came up over the horizon and the red glow of day broke over the tops of the trees. The birds and squirrels woke and made little scuffling noises in the dead brown leaves on the cold ground. Katie loved her time in the outdoors. This was prime time for hunting. The deer were all waking up too, and started to make their way out of their sleeping nests and into the clear-cuts, looking for something to eat. As Katie watched the day got lighter. She noted movement at the edge of the tree line only sixty-five yards away. Katie froze; she didn't even breathe, thinking that whatever it was might see her hot breath on the cold air.

Out of the trees walked three good-sized doe. Katie waited until they were all the way into the clearing. She stayed still until they all three lowered their heads to eat. Katie slowly pulled up the gun, sighted the largest of the three deer in her scope, took a slow breath, and then pulled the trigger. The sound of her .243 Remington rifle let everyone within earshot know that the young girl was going to go through the ritual of getting blooded for the first time that afternoon. Katie knew that the seasoned hunters around her could tell from the direction of the shot that the shot had to be young Katie who had fired. Katie was also one of the only hunters that used the smaller .243 Remington; the gun had a distinct sound that other hunters recognized.

Kate waited for twenty minutes, just like her dad had told her to do a hundred times, then slowly climbed out of the ladder stand and walked over to where the dead deer lay. She put the gun to its eye to make sure that it was dead, then let out a cry.

"Daddy!" Katie yelled. The sound broke the silence that always follows a gunshot on a hunting camp. After someone shot, everyone waited to see if another was taken, which was often the sign of a missed shot. From the other food plots came five distinct replies.

"What?" Five dads answered the call, just to be funny. Ten minutes later, Katie's dad drove up, smiling from ear to ear, feeling proud of his baby girl. Her dad being a little apprehensive himself about her new independence, had not gone very far away for the morning hunt. The minute he heard her shoot, he started toward her.

Several hours later, after the deer was cleaned and hung in the meat shed, Katie had a minute to think about what she had done. Everyone had celebrated her first kill. Katie enjoyed being the center of attention that was typical for a first kill, but the adrenaline was gone. Her mom had done the honor of wiping the deer's blood over her face. Looking at the pictures her mom had taken of Katie with her deer minutes before they had cleaned it, Katie realized that the fun of taking the deer was a means to an end. It was not the joy of killing a beautiful animal; it was the thrill of the hunt that made Kate plan to hunt again tomorrow. She thought that she should be sad for the deer or feel bad about killing something. She did not. It was hunting, nothing more, and nothing less. Hunting was a sport, and she knew that she enjoyed the sport of it.

As Katie had grown up she had continued to hunt, she had fallen in love with the sport. After learning to hunt deer, she had tried her hand at hunting ducks.

Duck hunting was very different, the gun was different and the shots were different. The setting and talent required was different. Katie needed to be a faster shot
to hunt ducks and other birds. She enjoyed duck hunting and added a few dove
hunts a year to her hunting resume. Dove were very fast moving, not flying in
predictable patterns, and Katie became a much better shot after a couple of dove
seasons. Adding the other types of hunting gave Katie more time in the woods
and increased her love of the sport as well as her ability. Katie had hunted in Alabama to start and then in Louisiana for dove hunts with friends several seasons.
In her twenties she and her parents had starting taking annual trips to Texas to
hunt white-tail and pigs. Katie had dated a guy who had a hunting camp in Mississippi and had been hunting with his family many times while they dated.

Katie had become a good hunter with many diverse animals to her credit. A
human being was a new one.

CHAPTER 3

▼

I saw a demonstration on TV once where this team of six people spent hours lining up thousands of dominos on this stage. The dominos went up ramps and down steps, thousands of them. When the team of people pushed the first domino, the fun started. The falling dominos pushed mechanical objects that made a windmill go around, which pushed another lever that struck a match and lit fireworks. These thousands of tiny little plastic rectangles make interesting patterns, made other objects move, and made the audience gasp and cheer. Everybody likes to be entertained and surprised by someone using something normal and making it do abnormal things. When the last domino fell, the camera shot the final results from high above the stage. The pattern was a perfect picture of the Statue of Liberty. It seemed that only the guys who laid out the dominos knew ahead of time what the end result will be. The audience was surprised and cheered the team's efforts.

This demonstration made me think about how the everyday things that happened to normal people are like these dominos. We all have these little pieces of normalcy that make up our lives. We all have events that are like these dominos. It's really hard to know when and how the dominos of someone's life start to fall. Is it destiny or do we push the first one ourselves? I believe that you can put two people in the same set of events, and, depending on how their dominos were lined up, these two individuals would have a different reaction to the events and different outcomes, different final pictures.

When those kids in Columbine, Colorado, decided to take guns into school with them that day and start shooting students and teachers, they didn't just get out of bed and go nuts, grab guns, long black coats, and head off to school. They had normal, everyday challenges—tests, grades, peer rejection—that they either couldn't handle or just chose not to handle in a normal way. Did they do it? Yes. Are they responsible? Yes. But their reality, their situation, made the final picture of dominos.

When normal people do amazing or horrible things, they don't just wake up one morning and do these things. Several years ago, a normal guy on his way to work, jumped out of his car, into a freezing cold river in Washington, and rescued several people who were drowning when a plane crashed into the river. There were a lot of normal things that happened to that guy to bring him to that day. When the dominos started to fall, your picture could be a good one or a bad one. How this final result manifested itself may be beyond our control.

It doesn't matter if people were talking about Hitler or Martin Luther King, we all have normal little situations and events in our lives that affect us without our realizing it until later. Two people given the same set of events will have different reactions and therefore a different outcome.

I was a perfect example of this; I could not control the events in my life. Be it God or Fate, I don't know what caused the events, but I chose the way I reacted to those events. I am responsible for the consequences of those reactions.

The individual dominos of my life seemed to be unremarkable. Heaven knows, for years, those separate issues were just a part of who I am, I was not particularly special. I'm just an average Southern gal. I am well over forty, single, no children, one cat. My only chance at children ended years ago in a stillborn baby girl. It was a heartbreaking event that I can't explain, nor could I make you understand even if I were to try. The fact that I couldn't have children drove me to want them even more and eventually led me to become a foster parent.

In my twenties, I was worried about my education and building a career; children were the furthest thing from my mind. I had plenty of time. I wanted to be stable before I had kids. Then one day, I woke up forty years old, divorced and childless, with no hope that I would ever be able to have them. The reality of what I had given up rocked my world more than I cared to admit. Another domino slowly fell over, landing squarely on the next one, silent to anyone standing close, but deafening to me.

Becoming a foster parent was the hardest, yet most rewarding, thing I ever did. I loved the kids and cared about what would happen to them long term. It was difficult to get through the process of qualifying as a foster parent and many times I wondered if it was worth it. I didn't really believe that I could make a difference at first. After several years as a foster parent I realized that we made a huge difference everyday. Being a foster parent to me was like walking on the beach and seeing thousands of starfish laying in the sand and dying. If you walked on by them, they would all surely die. Instead you could chose to pick the starfish up, one at a time and put them back into the water. You couldn't necessarily save them all before they died. But you could choose to save the ones you got to in time. Foster children were like these starfish. I could not save them all but the ones I got to, I could try to save. It was better than just standing back and feeling sorry for my situation of not having children. At least I was trying to help.

I supported myself and my foster children, not well, but I did okay. I was able to do pretty much everything I wanted to do. I made sure that the kids were taken care of and had decent clothes. I took a vacation once a year in some tropical place and owned my home. I've been working as a human resource manager for eighteen years and I was considered good at what I did. I've had two unsuccessful marriages before I became a foster parent, so I was a single foster parent from the beginning. When my mother's friend asked why a nice girl like me can't find a good man, I used the excuse that I'm "just not good at it." The "it" is being married and committed, the whole confusing nine yards. I had been single for over ten years. The truth was that it was even more difficult to find a man who understood why I would want to take on the responsibility of someone elses children when I didn't have to. More than one I heard from a boyfriend, "There not your kids, send them back." But I would rather have the kids in my life than the men, most times. I was happy with my life and my dominos the way they are.

I never looked at myself as unstable or damaged in any way. I don't think I'm someone who is lacking in anything. I liked my life, my work, my family, my friends. But just like real dominos, when you set them up just right in a row, and give the first one a little push, momentum starts a process where they all fall in an unexpected pattern. When the dominos of my life fell, the pattern ended up being something that I never imagined.

I've always believed that the great hand of God was the only thing responsible for laying out the dominos of my life. However, I'm honest enough with myself to believe that I am totally responsible for pushing some of the first dominos that changed my future forever. What I did can not be blamed on anyone else. Do I know what I did was wrong? Yeah, sure I do. Am I sorry for what I did? Not for a minute.

The picture that our dominos make may change everything we know about ourselves. Like when the dominos on TV fell down and the pattern was revealed from a camera shot high above the floor. The pattern you see makes you say "wow" or "Oh." I would like to think that to have a total change in your domino pattern or a total change in your morality; you would need an epiphany, some huge, earth-shattering event. In my case, it was as simple as walking to the mail box after a long, bad day at work.

I calmly opened the box and pulled out a notice from my local county courthouse. I recognized the name of the official on the envelope and knew instantly that I was summoned to jury duty. The dominos started to fall. Fate gently pushed the first one. Thinking back on it now, I think the dominos had been positioning themselves for a long time.

The dominos in my life so far could not totally explain what I had done. My childhood was normal and blessed, an overused description, but totally accurate in my case. I have two parents who have been married for almost fifty years and still look at each other as if the other was ice cream on a hot day in August. I had one brother who died when he was twenty-one years old in an accident. I was twenty at the time and lucky enough to understand that he was a good brother and a great friend. I still think about the injustice of it but know that it was just God's plan. He didn't have many dominos, but his ending picture was beautiful.

But now, I've lived more of my life without my brother than with him, so the pain of his loss was no excuse for my actions. All of this was background, not an excuse. Did my actions sometimes seem harsh? Yeah, I think they did. Did I have a tough shell around my heart? In some ways, we all have to have a hard shell in order to deal with the dominos of life.

I grew up in LA. That's Lower Alabama for those who confuse it with the one in California. I am not a Southern belle; I hunt, fish, cheer for the Tide, and scuba dive. What is a Southern belle? I don't know, it is hard to tell nowadays but I'm not a girly girl, drama queen. I watch NASCAR and drink beer so maybe I'm an educated redneck. I love Mardi Gras, which started in Mobile, Alabama, for those people who think incorrectly that the festival started in New Orleans. I'm normal with a normal childhood, normal education, and normal life—just normal—until I reported for jury duty and met Larry Cunningham.

I went to undergraduate and graduate school in New England to get away from where I had grown up in Alabama. I thought I wanted to see new things, meet different people. What I found was that the people were pretty much the same, regardless of the accents. I loved my time away from the south but chose to move back home to Mom and Dad and the friends I had known all my life.

Absolutely nothing about me would make you think that I am anything other than totally normal. I gave all the appearances of being a productive member of society. My parents and their friends described me as a good girl. Ex-boyfriends and ex-husbands described me as strong-willed and independent. Co-workers described me as hardworking and the kind of person who gets things done. I would never think of myself being described as a cold-blooded killer.

I knew from about five o'clock that morning that it would not be a good day. First, I worked in retail and today was inventory day. In less than forty-five minutes, all hell would break loose and sixty people who didn't speak English would descend on the store to count seven point two million dollars in nuts and bolts. I worked for the largest home improvement retailer in the world and inventory day is the worst day of the year in retail. I wasn't even completely in the door at work at six o'clock, when I was paged to pick up on lines one and two.

Line one was a nineteen-year-old lumber associate who was calling in (for the last time in his career with this company, I saw to that) to let me know that he understood this was one of the biggest days of the year for the store, but that he would not be able to make it in because, "I met a girl at the beach last night and I'm not coming in," regardless of what I thought or how much I pleaded with him to please come to work. This was what made me crazy, working in human resources. These people will beg for a job; you hire them thinking you've made a good choice. They tell you that you won't regret giving them a chance, giving them a break, or their first job. Then, within six months, they were acting like the front of the building should say "John's Home Improvement Store" not "THE Home Improvement Store."

Line two was my mother, who I love dearly, but who has no idea what it's like to organize the personnel to count over seven million dollars worth of nuts and bolts, and deal with these damn employees without a cup of coffee. She called every morning; some days she got me on my cell before I walk through the front door. This morning I moved too fast for her, and she missed me on my drive in, but got me in the store. My mother, bless her soul, loved to gossip about my friends, ex-boyfriends, her friends, and a pile of people I don't know but that I should know just because she knows them. She thought that the latest gossip about my ex-boyfriend from fifteen years ago was vital information at 6:00 a.m. Since she retired, she lived for this early morning gossip swaps, so I indulged her. I finished with both these calls, squared my shoulders and walked to the receiving area to meet the inventory counters who would decide our bonus payouts for the next year.

At the time, I had no idea that a bad day was going to go to toxic waste by eight that night. It ended up being a twelve-hour day, which wasn't that unusual for retail managers. I missed lunch again, also not unusual in human resources. The inventory was complete and the deed was done for another year. The numbers were okay, not great, but not terrible.

The final push of the dominos was when I got home and found the summons for jury duty waiting in the mail box. My first thought was, "Cool, this should be fun. Hearing all the stuff going on in the court system." My second thought was, "I should do my civic duty." My third was, "Yeah, I get to sit in a courtroom for a week and read a book. I don't have to go to work and listen to associate issues; it's a mini vacation in the making."

I was cordially invited to join two hundred other people to participate in the honor of jury duty.

CHAPTER 4

▼

The little community of Loxley, Alabama was just east of Mobile Bay, and south of I-10. The small community of fourteen hundred people was first settled in 1904 as a logging community. It was a small bedroom community between Mobile, Alabama and Pensacola, Florida. The largest employer was a flower company, but the largest majority of the residents, who have a median age of thirty seven and an annual income under thirty four thousand dollars a year, worked in either Mobile or Pensacola. Most folks knew Loxley as a two-stoplight town on Highway 59, on the way to the beaches of Gulf Shores and Orange Beach, Alabama. It was a great place to stop and get gas or visit the farmers market before getting to the high priced area of the beach.

It was a family focused town and hosted the annual Strawberry Festival each year in April. The biggest attraction for the festival was the Little Miss Strawberry contest, which selected a second grader from one of the schools in Baldwin County based on her poise, appearance, and personality. The coveted reigning queen was supported by a first runner-up and five royal court members. Loxley loved its children, and all the local churches supported the festival and the families. The one thing that Loxley wasn't short on was churches. The town had five churches in a five mile radius.

One of the oldest churches in the town was right on Highway 59, the Loxley Lutheran Church. It was a clear, bright morning when Larry Cunningham walked into the church at 7:00 a.m. on Sunday, April 4, with a smile on his face and a song playing in his head. Larry was humming the second song that the kids in the Lutheran Children's Choir would be singing that morning at the church service. Larry was a very busy, diligent and industrious man, but he liked to say that, "God gave him the energy and the kids gave him the joy."

Larry had been an active member of the Lutheran church since he was a child and had grown up an active member of the church family. He left town after high school, and nobody knew for sure where he went or what he was doing for the nearly ten years he was gone. Everyone assumed that he was away at school or working, but nobody really noticed, and his family never shared any information. Then, one Sunday five years ago, Larry reappeared in Loxley, a grown man. He just walked right into the Loxley Lutheran Church and sat down in the Cunningham family pew, as though he had never left. During the five years that he had been back in town, Larry worked hard for the church, volunteering for committees and organizing events. He helped repair the roof on the rectory after some hurricane damage, and he worked to get a freezer donated when the ladies of the church said they needed one for the kitchen. Now, he was the youth minister of the church, working with the kids several times a week. No one in town ever asked him anything about the time he was gone, and Larry never volunteered anything.

Larry's life was a well-planned and well-tended life. Wednesday was adult choir practice; Thursday was kid's choir practice; Friday was youth group night out; Saturday was the pancake breakfast fund-raiser every other week and, of course, Sunday was packed full of giving back to the Lord for the gifts he had given Larry. Sunday started with Junior Sunday school at nine o'clock, full church service at ten, and lunch with church members either in the rectory hall or at Flippers, a restaurant about a mile down the road and finally, Bible study at four.

Larry had been the youth minister for the church for three years. As the youth minister, Larry repeatedly told members of the church that he wanted to try new things to showcase the kids' talents, to develop the kids, and give them confidence. Larry told the parents that developing and expanding their kid's talents was a good way for him to give back to his community, and make the world a better place by creating responsible adults from the children of the church. Larry spoke to the board for the church many times, telling them that a well rounded child made a well rounded adult. Larry added that exposure to the arts, especially music added to the rounding out of a character.

Larry tried to introduce new things into the music of the church. It was Larry who gave permission to Jimmy Barnhill to play the guitar at church during the service. Coordinating the music with Mrs. Gilbert, who had been the organist for the last twenty years, was a negotiation that rivaled a Middle Eastern Summit. All the regular members of the church knew that Mrs. Gilbert did not play the guitar, did not approve of rock music, and did not approve of the use of instruments other than organs and pianos in the church. Larry was walking on sacred ground, and everyone in the church sat back to watch the fireworks. Getting Jimmy, age seventeen and Mrs. Gilbert, age seventy-one, together, was a major accomplishment for Larry. It took weeks of negotiations before Mrs. Gilbert would allow Jimmy to play just one song with her at a Wednesday night practice. Larry used all his charm to get Mrs. Gilbert to even consider changing her music. This was followed by weeks of additional rehearsals to get it right. If they were going to do this crazy new thing, then Mrs. Gilbert was going to make sure that it was perfect.

The final result was a true measure of the success. On a beautiful Easter Sunday, the duo played "Sweet Hour of Prayer" to open the service. The church was packed because everyone had heard that they had been practicing together and wanted to see the show. Nobody ever expected it to work except Larry, a self-proclaimed eternal optimist. They were to play two hymns that day. The first was a surprising success to everyone, but the second, "Jesus Don't Give Up On Me," was a grand accomplishment. There was not a person sitting when they finished, the entire church was on their feet, clapping with delight. Even Mrs. Barnhill, who was well over ninety but lied about her age, was part of the standing ovation. It had all worked out in the end, and the whole church was very impressed with the results and loved Larry all the more for keeping the faith.

Mrs. Gilbert and Jimmy continued to work together to provide the music for the church until Jimmy left Alabama when he graduated from high school. The boy now wrote music in Nashville for a small independent firm. Hometown boy made good. Larry liked to say that Jimmy was his shining star, the example of what he was trying to do in the church. The church members recognized Larry's efforts and supported his ideas with developing the kids.

Larry had a way of getting everyone to do things that they normally wouldn't ever dream of doing. Larry was an outgoing and good-looking man. He was five eleven, one hundred seventy-five pounds, and he had blond hair that turned just a little bit red during the summer months when he worked in his flower garden. His tan was perfect: no farmers tan, no sock lines. He had deep brown eyes like mocha coffee from Starbucks or a three-month-old puppy's eyes. He had a continuous smile on his pleasant face that was bright white and turned up just a little more on the right side than on the left side. His eyes were the first thing you noticed about his good looks but his smile was what kept people's eyes on him. His crooked smile was also helpful in entertaining the kids with funny faces when church got boring and they got fidgety, or if he wanted to wake them up before they sang. Larry wasn't just a good-looking guy; in this backwards small town of Loxley, Larry was hot for anywhere he might be living.

Larry was metro sexual before anybody in Loxley knew what that was. Larry was a great dresser; he was way too pressed and polished for the small farm town where jeans and dirty overalls were acceptable in most places. Larry was the kind of guy who ironed his jeans as well as his shirts and some members of the church didn't know how to take him at first. He ran around in tassel loafers when most of the male population of this town only had two pair of boots to their name. They had their dress boots and their hunting boots. Dress boots were for church; hunting boots were good for the rest of the days of the year, even when hunting season was months away. Larry dressed everyday as if it was Sunday and this concerned the farmers in the church who believed that the only way to tell if somebody was a hard workers was to look at their dirty fingernails.

Larry was great for the kids because he set a new standard for them and pushed them to wear clothes that fit, not the oversized jeans that hung off their butts. He made sure that the kids did not wear t-shirts with off-color saying on them and that the young girls did not wear dresses or shorts that were of unacceptable length. Larry didn't let the kids wear baseball caps inside, not even for youth group events, and he made sure that everyone remembered their "yes, sirs" and "no, sirs." The moms really appreciated his efforts, understanding that Larry was helping grow good future adults.

He had also been a source of interest for the single women in the church, as he was one of few single men at the church. Larry had a quick wit and a compliment for every woman from age eight to eighty. Larry's favorite hobby was gardening and he was uncanny at remembering the ladies' favorite flowers. Larry remembered everyone's birthday in the church with at least a card, but the ladies always got flowers. He was a ladies' man, the type of guy who actually noticed a new hair cut the first time he saw you, not two weeks later, like most guys. Most guys have to be asked, "Do you notice anything different?" before they would even look hard at a woman. Larry was the type that noticed without any prompts. As if all of this wasn't enough to drive the church ladies crazy, Larry was also smart and sweet.

He was a true Southern gentleman with all the ladies. He had never asked a single one of the church ladies out. And, on the many occasions when they had invited him to parties or Mardi Gras balls, he had respectfully declined, often making up previous engagements to not hurt their feelings. This actually worked to make the single ladies of the church chase him harder.

Larry's real job as fireman for the city of Robertsdale was another hot quality. During the week, Larry wore a uniform that turned heads and stopped hearts.

A couple of years before, he became the small town hero when Mrs. Barnhill who was in her late eighties at the time, tripped in her kitchen while frying chicken and broke her ankle. The spatter from the grease had made the floor in front of the oven slippery and she had fallen. She was still cooking when it happened she had not taken the grease off the stove, so within minutes it caught fire and spread quickly from the kitchen to the den. Larry happened to be driving down by on his way home from work and saw the smoke. He got on his cell phone and notified the station, then went straight into Mrs. Barnhill's house without waiting for the fire truck. By the time, the truck with help arrived, Larry had carried the elderly lady out of the house in her day dress and sat her in a porch swing tied to a tree in the front yard. Larry was an instant Hometown Hero.

As happens in small towns, the ladies of the town made sure that Larry was invited for dinner at absolutely everyone's house for the next several weeks. The kids also thought Larry being a fireman was cool. In all respects, Larry had it going on. No doubt about it.

Larry told members of the church that he loved his work as the youth minister. The Loxley Lutheran Church was no different from any other Southern church in this day and age. It had an abundance of single women of all ages and a score of middle-aged, single mothers. There was more time spent discussing Larry Cunningham than the weather in hurricane season. Though everyone knew that Larry was a hot commodity in this particular market, he played it very cool, never falling for the flirty comments by the ladies. He helped out many of the single moms when father/son duty was required but no father was available. Everyone noticed that he attended little league games and band recitals. The ladies gossiped endlessly about how Larry made sure that he was there for soccer practice. He even volunteered to teach one church member's son to drive after the boy's mother had failed to get him ready for his driving test. He was the first one to the hospital when tonsils had to come out and the last one to leave when any of the kids had a birthday party. Larry loved the kids of his church, and the parents thought the world of him, too.

In Baldwin County, in order to get a child out of school, you had to have advance permission from a legal guardian. Larry was authorized to check out almost any of the church kids from school, a privilege reserved for select relatives in most cases. He was the one you called when you needed to take the kids to the dentist but didn't have any time to take off of work. Larry was the guy who came to fix your lawn mower or hang a ceiling fan. He replaced lights on outside fixtures when you couldn't get them without a ladder. And mostly, he was there for everything having to do with "his kids." Larry was regularly told that he would make a great father. Most of these comments came from the single ladies in the church who fantasized that he would pick them as his girlfriend.

Larry did understand the limits to his position as the youth minister, so he made it a rule never to date any of the mothers of his kids. He was upfront with the ladies in the church and let them know that he just couldn't cross that line. The moms said that this was a reflection of his true and pure spirit in a life given to God's work. What really got to the ladies of the church, those Southern belles born under the magnolia leaves, was the deep baritone voice that they heard every Sunday. It was a voice that could melt chocolate sitting in a six-foot snow drift in Maine in January. When Larry sang solos on Sunday, the Daughters of the Confederate would cross their legs to keep their minds on the fact that they were in the house of God. When these ladies got together for ballgames or school functions, Larry was the favorite topic of conversation. The ladies of the church spend countless hours discussing everything Larry. How he dressed, how he lived, what he believed and, mostly, why he wasn't married.

It seemed that Larry knew he had this effect on the ladies but that didn't do a thing in the world to keep him in his seat at the front of the church. He sang for the love and duty to God, not to anyone of this earth. He understood the effect he had on women, heaven knows he was not that naive, but he didn't acknowledge it publicly, not even to his brother, the church minister.

On this Sunday, as always, Larry was the first to arrive at church. He generally arrived before his brother, Tim, who had been the minister for several years, to get the coffee going and set out the hymnals. It was important to Larry that everyone in the choir had the hymnals on the seats so they had a marked copy with the new red leather cover. The small church was not able to buy enough copies of the new red leather covered hymnals last year. Form and appearance being vital to presentation by the choir, collecting and setting up the matching hymnals was the first thing he did every Sunday morning. The church planned to buy another twenty-five this year, but for now, he wanted to make sure that when the choir members stood up and held their hymnals in front of them to sing, the presentation was consistent and planned. He smiled to himself and said of his favorite phrases. "The devil is in the details." How true, how true.

"Good Morning, Larry," yelled Jennifer Kollman as she stepped into the church rectory. She carried a tray of fresh-baked gingerbread men for after-church coffee. Jennifer was one of Larry's favorites, or so he told her, and a very attractive lady at that.

Jennifer had been a member of the church for two years, and she was now its community service director. She was thirty-eight and had long, blond, straight hair and the body of someone who had too much on her plate and no time to eat. Jennifer told her best friend, Jamie, that she was tired of working hard so hard and that she had not been laid in so long that she wondered what was wrong with her. She worked hard at taking good care of herself both physically and spiritually. When she divorced her husband and the father of her son, she had told her friends that she needed a change of scenery. With family near Loxley, it seemed like the place to relocate to after years in Atlanta.

Jennifer lusted after Larry like the rest of the women in the town, but she was smart enough to realize that either Larry was not interested in any of them, or he was more discreet than any of them knew. Nobody ever saw him out on the town when he wasn't with one of the kids from the church. They had never seen him drinking or even having dinner a date. When she first joined the church, she was amazed that the church had so many single moms as members. After a month, she told Jamie that she was thankful she had had found these single moms. They had all become instant friends and a great support system for her. She had told them all that it was an advantage to have like souls around you. She felt like she stood out in other churches she had visited before, but this small church and the other mothers, gave her the feeling of family. She liked the fact that this church did not condemn or judge them as failures for being divorced. They all agreed, but what they didn't like was that they were all very lonely for good male companionship.

Larry was never linked romantically with anyone that the church ladies knew of, but they had hundreds of conversations about why he didn't have a girlfriend. Nobody was buying the "it would not be right for the kids" song that Larry sang. Jamie's opinion was that Larry had a girlfriend in Mobile that he never brought around. Nancy said that she thought that his heart had been broken severely several years ago and he hadn't recovered which was a romantic idea but had no evidence of fact.

The men of the church whispered that the guy must be gay; what other possible reason could there be for him not taking advantage of so much easy tail? The married guys and the couple of single men in the church watched all these women, watch Larry. They watched the church ladies playing to Larry and listened as they all tried to flirt with him. It was a sport to see which one of these lonely ladies would priss up to him with their latest come-and-get-me dresses on to try to get his attention. It was a game, and these men spend hours wondering why they didn't get to play. While the women in the church spent time wondering what they could do to get Larry's attention, the men in the church spent time wondering why the dumb ass wasn't taking advantage of a different one of them each night. The guys had hundreds of conversations about Larry being gay. What other explanation could there be, unless he was gay? Problem was, even the guys liked Larry. They should have hated the guy because of their jealousy, but they actually liked him instead. He was funny and bright. He liked sports and could fix anything that happened with a car or a home appliance. The guy would help you do anything.

Larry had just finished turning down the air conditioner over the choir loft. The main church building was old, and the congregation had added a new air conditioning unit to the front of the church a couple of years ago. The result was that the choir loft in the front of the church could be hot as hell while the church members in the back of the church could be freezing. The result was a constant battle to keep everyone happy. The two separate units weren't operated by the same controls, and it was Larry's responsibility to make sure that the choir had the air turned on in advance so they weren't sweating during their performance. Larry had stated that he hated when it got hot this time of year and he could see his choir sweat from the front rows of the congregation. Details, details, details.

"Good Sunday Morning, Lady Jennifer," Larry called back in a James Bond voice as he moved to the organ to make sure Mrs. Gilbert's music was set out. "What tortuously delightful treats have you made for us poor souls who are watching our weights today?" The smell of baked goods came from the plate that Jennifer brought in with her.

"Gingerbread men for the general population and chocolate pecan cookies for you, Larry," she replied, beaming and holding the plate of cookies covered in plastic wrap up for his review. "And you know you don't need to watch your weight, you're perfect." Jennifer turned away and rolled her eyes; she couldn't believe that she had just said that out loud.

She had been a very successful mortgage banker in Atlanta, and had moved away from a high-paying job to give her only child, Jacob, a chance at growing up in a place that wasn't filled with school children selling crystal meth in the locker rooms. Jacob was her top priority, always had been, and always would be. Jennifer had proven herself in a male-dominated business. She and Jacob's father had gotten married to seal a business deal themselves. They worked together several times in business and started dating each other because they were too busy to find anybody outside of work to spend time with. Their marriage had been great at the beginning. They were both building careers, working their way up in large firms. Their problem was outside of business, they had very little in common.

Jennifer told her girlfriends that she had gotten pregnant and Jacob had changed everything. With the new baby, Jennifer made the decision that family was more important than her career, and even though she continued to work, she lost the hard-charging focus that she had shown in business prior to Jacob's birth. She spent more time with Jacob and tried to get Jacob's father to do to the same. Jacob's father had tried to give his son the attention he knew he needed, but he was not the father that he needed to be, and his heart just wasn't into it. His heart was into making money.

Jacob, eleven years old, came through the door behind his mom carrying the second tray of cookies. He had grown into a good-looking kid; he was a little skinny even for his age and a little on the tall side. He had blond hair and took after his mom. Jacob didn't seem as unsure of himself as the other kids in his school; he seemed self-reflective without being self-absorbed. The girls at school had started to notice him this year, but he had not yet begun to notice them. Jacob was a boy's boy and would probably grow to be a man's man, or so his mother told her friends.

Jennifer hadn't once regretted the move to the small town in Alabama. Her friends knew that she owned a good mortgage business; she had parents close by to help with Jacob; and, up until this year, Jacob seemed to love everything about the move to the slower pace and a smaller school. He had gone from a small fish in a large pond of an inner city school to a big fish in the small pond of Central Baldwin County School. Jacob was a good looking kid who had a big city reputation with the kids at school since he was from Atlanta. This made the other kids think that he knew more about the ways of the world than they did, and in a small town, that was a source of power when you were eleven.

About two months ago, Jennifer had noticed a change in her happy-go-lucky kid, and she talked to Pastor Tim about the change in Jacob. She said that something was going on with Jacob. His grades had fallen from the straight A's of last year to low B's and C's this year. He also seemed to be spending too much time in his room. She had hooked up his new computer in his room with the internet, so maybe that was it. He seemed to enjoy that computer more than his friends lately. She told Pastor Tim that as soon as she got one minute to sit still and talk to Jacob they needed to try to figure out what was up with that kid of hers. Just being eleven probably, Pastor Tim replied. She wondered if all eleven-year-olds were moody and introverted one minute, happy and extroverted the next. Hormones! Ugh!

"Anything interesting on the song list for today, Larry?" Jennifer questioned, trying to recover from the "perfect" comment. She was always doing that, saying things to Larry and regretting them immediately. The great thing about Larry was he never once acknowledged the flirty comments that any of the gang of girls threw at him. Jennifer watched what she said, not wanting to come off as flirting with him, but the others didn't even try to hide their lust for him. Larry was the hot commodity for the two stop light town and probably the only reason most of the ladies never missed a Sunday at church.

"'I Believe For Every Drop Of Rain' and 'God Be With You Till We Meet Again,' both performed to Grammy Award–winning standards by our kids' choir. You know several of them have real talent," Larry said.

"One of my favorites," replied Jennifer.

Even the worst singers were given opportunities to sing either in the choir or solos. Larry had told several parents that in order to develop kid's confidence and make stronger adults, performing in front of the church family was a good building block. Larry liked to say that if you got them out in front of people, early and often, they had a better chance of finding their confidence and being more successful later in life. He also said that no matter how short on talent a kid might be, your church family never laughs or condemns, at least not until they got back in their cars going home after church. This made the church a safe environment for kids to experiment and find out if they did have talent.

"Morning, Jacob," said Larry. "You excited about singing today?"

"Yes, sir," Jacob answered with more formality than necessary.

Jennifer wondered again, what is up with that kid of mine?

"You'll do just fine," Larry said to Jacob "You did a great job at practice this week. I really appreciate you helping with the other kids. You know son, you show great leadership ability with your peers. These are great qualities for your future."

Jennifer ruffled Jacob's hair, "Say thank you Jacob" she directed.

"Thanks Larry" Jacob said looking at his feet.

"Kids" Jennifer sighed.

"Kids" echoed Larry.

The back door of the church slammed with a loud bang before Larry could continue. In walked Shawn and Kevin, the Evans brothers. Shawn was eleven years old and Jacob's alter ego. Where Jacob was kind and controlled, Shawn was brash and reckless. Where Jacob was blond and skinny, Shawn was dark and stocky. If given an easy way to do something, Jacob would always take it. Shawn, on the other hand, would play the rebel and fight to make things harder than they needed to be. These were the differences that made the boys best friends. Shawn was a fighter, Jacob was a negotiator. If given the opportunity, Jacob would talk the situation out and get everyone to calm down. Shawn was lit dynamite with a short fuse. If they were in an old western, Jacob would have worn a white hat and Shawn would have worn a black hat.

Shawn and Jacob met when Jacob moved to town and enrolled in school. Shawn had immediately tested him, trying to intimidate the new kid, which was only one of his hobbies. It only took once for them to get nose to nose for both boys to understand that they really liked each other and didn't need to fight. From that moment on, they were rarely on opposite sides of any issue. They both understood at that young age that they were stronger together as friends and weaker as adversaries.

"Hey, Mr. Larry!" Kevin shouted. He was eight and the youngest of the clique of boys in the kid's choir. "Shawn said I'm going to mess everything up this morning, but I told him he's a jerk. And Mom said he was jinxing me and that if he didn't shut up that he couldn't go to the camp with us next weekend. Shawn said that my voice was going to crack because I'm still a baby. Mom said that I'm not a baby." Kevin said in a breathless stream of nerves and excitement. Kevin would sing two frames by himself this morning. He'd been practicing for weeks with the kid's choir and still did "crack" occasionally, but Larry was willing to give it a shot. Kevin, even at his young age, told everyone that Larry was the greatest because of this huge show of faith by Larry.

"I did not say 'shut up', I told him to hush," called Jamie Evans, Shawn and Kevin's mom, from somewhere in the back of the church. Jamie, a forty-year-old single mom was a twenty-first century hippie. The boys' father had tired of his hippie throwback wife and walked out on all of them, and into a new condo with a Hooter's waitress two years ago. Jamie, who had told Jennifer that nobody over twenty-five looked good in those shorts, had taken this totally in stride and continued to wear long, flowing gauze dresses, burned incense, and still occasionally smoked a little pot. She never smoked in front of the boys though; she was a better mother than that.

Jennifer had told Jamie that she respected that she worked so very hard not to bad mouth her ass of an ex-husband to the boys, which was hard to do after everything he had done. Jamie told her that Shawn had taken it hardest and had become a little bully to vent the anger that he could not vent at his dad. Both boys had trouble with school for a couple of months after their father left, but Jamie told her that Larry had helped and they seemed back on track. The boy's father still came around every second or third weekend and took them to

Hooter's for hot wings. Shawn told his mom that he hated these trips and made a big play of leaving the messiest table possible, knowing that Sondra, the new girl-friend, would have to clean it up. Jamie's ex-husband had told her that Sondra had asked her new boyfriend not to bring the kids back in Hooters, but just like a lot of older guys with younger trophy girlfriends who worked where drinkers hung out, he spent a lot of time in the restaurant watching her work. Taking his kids to Hooter's was just another excuse for going in there.

"I'm sure you'll do fine, Kevin," said Larry, hoping to calm his frayed nerves. "We had several great practices the last couple of weeks and you're going to be great."

"Thanks, Larry. Look, I have a new shirt on. Mom bought it for today. She says that I need to look my best when I'm in front of the church. Shawn says that a new shirt won't make up for my ugly face and my pig nose. Mom says that I got my nose from my dad and that if I don't like it, I can blame his side of the family. Shawn says that I should have worn my Hawaiian shirt and then nobody would have noticed that I'm ugly." Kevin was more hyper than a new puppy on speed.

"Kevin, you'll be fine. Now calm down and leave Larry alone," called Jamie. She walked to the back of the church.

As it got closer to the service, the church began to fill up. There was a standard order to church service seating. It was actually a two-step process. First, the stan-dard seating area for the big families in the church and second, everybody else. The Barnhills always sat on the right side of the church, row twelve. The Martins sat on the left side: row seven adults, row six kids. The Duvalls took the right side, row four. People talked about the Duvalls because they guessed that the rea-son for sitting closer to the front of the church was due to Uncle Joe Duvall turn-ing to drugs after he lost all that money selling real estate. The real reason was that Granddaddy Duvall couldn't hear well but refused to let anyone know who wasn't immediate family.

Heaven help your soul if you were new to the church and made the mistake of sitting in a designated family seat. You could be sure that the next Sunday, they would be here before you so you didn't get their family plot. The most common ploy was to have your kids leave Sunday school early and plop themselves in the seats to save for the adults. Status was everything in a small town church, and this one was no different. It had become such an issue that one Sunday, Brother Tim had done the full sermon on welcoming new people into the church, and that it didn't matter where members were sitting as long as they were inside. The ser-mon was good, and everybody took it to heart. For the next two weeks, every-body made a big show of sitting in a different area of the church than where they normally sat. Two weeks later, they were back to marking their territory like neighborhood dogs.

At exactly five minutes after the hour, Brother Tim walked into the church behind the Thompson twins who would light the candles in the front of the church this morning. They proceeded to the opening hymn; Larry led in the choir loft. The adult choir always sounded great, so Larry stood before them, eyes closed, arms directing the flow as the music that God gave, drifted out over the congregation and through the open windows. It was another perfect day to serve God.

The first item on the agenda was always Announcements. This was a time for everyone to let you know how busy they were working for the church, and for making you feel guilty because you weren't pulling your weight. This, hopefully, made you feel guilty enough to help them. A number of the members had announcements: who was sick, who had children going overseas or returning from overseas on military duty, or whose great aunt twice removed had died and needed your prayers. Larry always waited until the last announcement to give an update on any kid's events. This Sunday was no different.

"Anybody know what happens next weekend?" he asked innocently enough. Of course they knew! They'd been planning and waiting for three months for a summer camping weekend to come along. Every kid and parent in the building started to cheer. The kids, because it promised to be fun camping, swimming, playing baseball, making crafts, and cooking out on an open fire. The parents cheered because they were getting rid of the kids for the four-day weekend. They all cheered Larry because he was the guy that made it happen for both groups.

"Okay, don't forget that I gave everyone a list of the required items that each of you must bring: sleeping bags, bug spray, flashlight, clean socks, and any special medicinal items. Darren, don't forget your inhaler this year; we were all the way to Atmore when you remembered last year. Parents, please pack a little less candy. They were all wired for sound three nights last year. I like to never have gotten the monsters to sleep with all the M&M's running through their veins." Everyone laughed because they knew Larry was serious. He loved this four-day trip more than the kids. Planned all year long and every year it was a little bit better. Thanks be to God and Larry Cunningham.

As the service went on, the kids' choir did an excellent job. All the practice and effort by Larry had paid off. Kevin did an outstanding job, holding his own for his solo. Even Shawn clapped when the song was over and ruffled his hair when he sat back down. Kevin would be beaming for days, now that everyone seemed to love him. Everyone said that they would keep Larry in their prayers. "Thank you God for his patient and self-sacrificing man. Keep him sane in spite of our brats."

CHAPTER 5

▼

Camp Hope was a good place for the kids to be during the early spring in south Alabama. When the camp started in August 1961, it was originally designed as a Boy Scout camp but a lack of funds, and a decline in the number of scouts in the area had caused other clubs and church groups in the county to pay a small membership usage fee to spend time at the camp. This allowed the owners of the camp to afford the upkeep, and the groups all got their turn. It also gave the camp a more diverse population of campers, which meant that during the school year they had other campers on the weekends. Camp Hope was a south Alabama, young redneck version of time-sharing for underage campers.

The camp sat on a small lake and originally had only tents. In 1979, twelve small cabins were built, and the tents were removed. The cabins were set up in three groups of four cabins each, which the camp directors referred to as pods. Each pod had a different tree name: oak, poplar, maple or southern pine. For kids this mattered; nobody wanted to be a poplar tree. There was nothing cool about a poplar tree. When the kids arrived and got off the bus, there was a run to the cabins in the Oak section for first dibs. The Oak pod was closest to the lake but the farthest away from the counselors' cabins. The three groups of four cabins were only fifty yards apart, but who got in your group of cabins was vital to your social status. You wanted to make sure that you had all your friends in the four adjoining cabins. This made moving from cabin to cabin easier during the day, and after hours when the lights were out.

Each cabin slept eight campers. There were four sets of metal bunk beds in each cabin. Because the cabins were now twenty years old and the funding was limited, these were not high-tech construction units. When it rained, the cabins leaked. When the bugs were bad, they were inside with you. The floors of the cabins were plywood with no carpet on them. It was best to keep your socks on all the time because you had no idea what was crawling on the floor.

Camp Hope started in the days when being a Boy Scout was something that guys did to learn how to survive outdoors and cook over an open fire. This was before being a Boy Scout became a political statement. It was when the Boy Scouts were about building characters of young men and not defining the sexual orientation of the adults who just wanted to help raise good strong members of society.

Along with the tents and later cabins, Camp Hope built a central clubhouse where kids and their leaders could sit together after a long day of canoeing and building bird houses to praise God, and eat grilled hamburgers and homemade potato salad. The clubhouse was better maintained than the individual cabins. The clubhouse was two thousand square feet of open space except for the kitchen area, which was separated by a wall with large open windows to the main hall. Its twenty-foot ceiling gave it an even larger feel. The food was prepared in the kitchen, and counselors could see out into the main hall through the long open windows to the main hall. The windows were constructed with countertops on them so they served as a buffet area for the kids to line up and get their meals. It kept the kids out of the kitchen but gave the counselors an open view of what the campers were doing while the counselors tried to cook in peace.

At the front of the hall, ran a long wooden table the counselors used. Kids were not allowed at the head table. The main hall included twenty-foot-long homemade wooden picnic tables where kids ate their meals. Two bathrooms were opposite the kitchen. The walls were old tongue and groove that had never been painted. The neatest thing about the clubhouse was that the walls were decorated with framed pictures of the all the years of campers who had come through Camp Hope.

There were pictures of kids, who, twenty years ago, had jumped off the pier and into the lake. There were pictures of kids in canoes, who were now grown up and had kids of their own who came through Camp Hope. For the returning campers and several adults who had been to the camp before, the pictures were conversation starters with new friends and old. Adults, who now paid for their children to come to the camp, spent hours looking at the old photos and pointing out themselves to their kids.

Years before, a spillway had been built on the south side of the lake where the lake overflowed into a smaller pool of crystal clear, cold water. Each set of campers built small boats out of plastic banana split containers from Dairy Queen and made paper for sails during their arts and crafts time. Then, on the last night at Camp Hope, everyone went down to the lake and placed a tea candle in their boat, each one named and decorated by the campers. The candles were lit, and the boats were placed in the water at the top of the spillway and set sail. The natural flow of the lake took the sailboats down the spillway and into the small reflecting pool below. It was a beautiful view, fifty or sixty boats flowing down the lake. Kids remembered the ceremony for the rest of their lives.

Camp rules were that the lights, controlled by a generator, went out at 10:00 p.m. For forty years at Camp Hope, when the generator was turned off, one of the kids had a flashlight that became the central source of light for memorable conversations about all the stuff your parents didn't want you talking about. The campers all thought that they were getting away with something, trying to hide the flashlight glow by putting blankets over the cabin windows. But the counselors knew what was going on and let the kids have their fun for an extra hour or two. If they noticed the flashlights on after about eleven thirty, then the counselor banged on the cabin wall and scared the shit out of the kids so they would turn out the light and go to sleep. From a counselor's perspective the trick was to wear the kids out during the day so they passed out at night.

The older kids from Loxley Lutheran church had been successful in getting all of them in the same cabin. That had been planned for months. They were also successful in running like jaguars and getting the cabin that they wanted in the Oak section of the camp. Oak was the best because they had recently been renovated, and had newer floors in them that didn't creak when you walked across them.

It was the first night of the camp, and Jacob, the leader of the group, one of the oldest and the best planners remembered his flashlight from previous visits. Just after ten o'clock, he reached in his knapsack and pulled out the large black Maglite with eight fresh D batteries his mom had bought him for the trip. Jacob always knew what to do and gave the other orders on how to get the cabin ready so the counselors wouldn't fuss for a while.

"Cover the windows Shawn," he instructed to get ready. "Everybody sit still a minute until we get everything in place." Jacob was a natural leader; he was the guy who remembered sandwiches when they went fishing at the creek. He was the one who made sure that everyone checked their tires before they started out on a bike ride. Jacob was the guy who thought of everything when they came to Camp Hope; he always had an extra toothbrush or socks. If you needed it, Jacob probably had it.

"Everybody stay put for a minute until I get this thing set up," he said to the seven other guys in the cabin. For a second, in total blackness, the boys waited while Jacob rigged a flashlight holder to hang from under one of the bunk beds like a chandelier. The trick was to keep it from swinging after you got it tied up because the light would make scary shapes on the walls when it was moving.

A loud bump came from over by the window and everybody jumped. "Damn it," said Shawn. "Crap!"

"You okay, Shawn?" asked Jacob, still messing with the flashlight and trying to hurry. "Hang on, I almost got it." Jacob was also the only one other than Shawn who was tall enough to rig the light up.

"No problem, I just stubbed my foot on the bed post over here," he responded. "That hurt."

"That's why he told you to sit down, dumbass," Darren said. Darren, always the follower, never the leader, did what he was told. Darren had the intelligence to be a leader, he just lacked the motivation. He believed he should be Jacob's number two man, but he knew that Shawn was second in command, and Darren couldn't find the motivation for a power play either. Darren was a go-with-the-flow kind of guy. The rest of Darren's life would probably be the same.

"Kiss this," Shawn said, pulling down his sweatpants and mooning Darren in the low light of the camp. This caused an explosion of laughter from everyone followed by everyone"hushing" everyone else at the same time.

"Man, that's the whitest ass I have ever seen" said Chris.

"Except for that big huge mole on the right cheek" added Darren

"Uglyest I've ever seen" said Doug.

"Shut up, guys. You want to get every counselor, including Larry, down here?" Chris said, as he pulled his pillow into his lap and crossed his legs Indian style.

The boys went to school together, they had known each other their whole short lives, and their moms couldn't wait to get rid of them for this long week-end. All the boys were the products of single-parent families; some of them had been without dads for their whole lives: others, like Jacob, for a relatively for a short period of time. The involvement with their fathers differed for each boy; some saw their dads every other weekend. A couple, like Jacob, hadn't seen their fathers in months. Shawn and Chris had the added issue of having little brothers who were also part of the group. Nothing was as uncool as having your little brother hanging around all the time.

"The guy's a jerk! And that's all there is to it," said Jacob, in a continuation of the early dinner conversation about Larry Cunningham.

Unlike any other conversation this group had ever had, this one brought them all to silence. These guys had grown up like brothers; they were family. They would fight each other in a minute, choosing sides every time. The same group wasn't always on the same side, but everyone always had an opinion. And like family, everyone heard each other's opinion even when they pretended that they didn't. This time the discussion was different. Jacob had been on a roll since dinner and showed no sign of letting up until he got it all out.

He seemed to have an important point to make, but nobody, not even his best friend and the strongest of the group, Shawn, wanted to have this conversation. Shawn thought he knew that something important was on Jacob's mind and just couldn't stop himself.

"What do you mean, Jacob? Larry is the man, dude. He's the reason we're here. He's the guy who helped out Darren's mom when she had to move out in the middle of the night because his dad went crazy. He's the one who got Keith out of trouble with the principal when he got caught with his dad's cigarettes. Larry's the guy that my mother says is the most eligible bachelor in Loxley. Whatever that means. I think all our moms have a crush on the guy." Shawn started out with a calm voice, but it was a snarl by the time he finished his last word.

"They were my mom's boyfriend's cigarettes, not my dads" said Keith.

Over dinner, Jacob had in a whispered tone he had asked each of the boys what they really thought of Larry. It was obvious that something big was happening here as the others watched Jacob, who was pacing now. Jacob was badmouthing Larry, Shawn was getting his "I need to hit something" tone, which really wasn't that unusual, but Jacob badmouthing Larry? Now that was front-page news.

"He ain't so great is all I'm saying. Sure, my mom thinks he's great, but hell, so does your mom, Darren. Everybody thinks this guy is the greatest thing since duct tape. Well … he's not, and I think if you guys'll just be real about this, you'll know it," begged Jacob. "They don't know," he said, pointing off into the darkness beyond the cabin door as if the other campers were right outside. "But I think maybe you guys might know it, and you're just too chicken shit to admit you think so, too." His voice cracked.

The guys were scared now; none of them would look up at Jacob except Shawn, who obviously had no idea what was going on in the cabin tonight.

Jacob went on, "If you guys know how crazy this guy is, you'd probably have stayed home instead of coming here this weekend. The guy is a nut job … youth minister, my ass!" He started crying.

The boys were really scared. If asked, they wouldn't have been able to tell which was scarier: the direction of the conversation or the fact that their leader was crying. As the tears rolled down his young, pale face, he looked much older than his eleven years. The guys all sat in total shock, staring at Jacob. Jacob was not just their leader, he was their north star. He was the bond that kept them together during divorces, mother's boyfriends that they hated, teachers who didn't care that the past weekend was a kid's one chance in three months to see his dad. And seeing Dad was a lot more important than your stupid math homework. Jacob was the only rock-solid mentor that these kids had other than their moms.

Jacob had carried Doug home when he broke his ankle two years before while he was showing off for some redheaded girl at the beach. Jacob had reported those bullies from Robertsdale Middle School when they started the fight at the county softball tournament. He probably saved Shawn's life that night because it had been Shawn's mouth that escalated the whole thing. If Shawn would have keep out of the conversation and let Jacob handle it, the middle school bullies wouldn't have wanted to kick his butt. To watch Jacob lose it like this was a blow to their infrastructure as third and fourth graders.

"Look guys," Jacob said, calmer now, "some stuff has happened, and I'm thinking you guys may already know about it. I'm asking without asking about what you guys know." He stopped, took a deep breath, and closed his eyes. "Larry Cunningham is a liar, and he does things to kids he shouldn't do. I know he does things because he did it to me a little over a year ago. And I know that he did it to at least one of you guys just last weekend. Man, if you guys know what I'm talking about, you've got to be straight with me. You've got to help me stop him. They'll never believe just one kid if I report him myself."

"What kinds of things?" asked Shawn. Shawn stood in the middle of the tent, his arms spread wide. Everyone else was still seated on the bunk beds like they had been told to do.

"Man, it's the stuff Coach Randall warned us about in health class. I didn't listen when they were talking to us last year, but now I'm freaked out. Larry touched me, dude! And he's touched at least one more of us, but I think we may all know something, so, if we stick together, they'll believe us." It all came out in an uncontrollable rush of words that Jacob seemed unable to stop. Once it was all out, he opened his eyes and looked from face to face.

"You're crazy, Jacob! Totally nuts! Where do you get this stuff from?" Shawn asked. "You been reading all those books of yours, and now you've made up this crazy story in your head, and nobody is going to believe you." He balled up his fists like he was ready to fight. Shawn's reaction to anything he did not understand was anger.

"No, Shawn, it's true," said the small, thoughtful, scared voice of Kevin. He was the youngest of the boys by four months and Shawn's little brother. "I was the one who went to Jacob the other day. After church last weekend, Larry gave me a ride home, remember? On the way home he said he had to stop by his house to get something for Mom. He said it would just take a minute and that I should come inside with him. When we got inside, he asked if I needed to use the bathroom. I said yeah, and he showed me where it was. So, I'm in there and Larry's standing there watching me. When I was finished, he said he needed to look at my thingy. Said it didn't look right to him. So I turned around, and at first he just held it in his hand, but then …" Kevin started to cry.

"For real?" asked Shawn

"Yes, for real" answered Kevin

Shawn knew his mom's third ex-boyfriend had whipped Kevin with a belt until Kevin had red marks that Shawn thought would never go away. His mom had thrown the guy out after that and moved on to boyfriend number four. Kevin was changed by that incident. He became quieter and less playful. He would sit in the room all alone and stare off into space. When he noticed someone there, he'd jump like he had seen a ghost. He had trouble with school and just couldn't concentrate. Shawn had wanted to kill the guy, but Mom had told the boyfriend to get lost and he just left, leaving Shawn angry again without any outlet for the anger.

Shawn stopped when he heard his little brother. Nothing moved except his eye muscles as he stared at Kevin, then Jacob, then Kevin again. Shawn blinked, his mouth hanging open like a bass waiting for a fly.

"What are you talking about, Kev? You're eight. What do you know about this pervert stuff?" Shawn asked, growing louder now. "Larry's your buddy. When boyfriend number three beat you to within an inch of your life, it was Larry who came over that night. Remember? It was Larry who stopped Mom from crying and Larry who took you to the doctor the next day. It was Larry, ya'll! Larry! Not some pervert—Larry. Our Larry!"

"He's not my Larry, Shawn," answered Mikey's little voice from behind Shawn. "The dude is a freak, man. He tells ya stuff and gets you to do stuff, a little at a time. 'Here, do this, and I'll talk to your mom about your grades.' 'Do that and I'll make sure the coach lets you play in the Little League game Saturday.' 'You know I love you like my own son, so this needs to be our secret. Nobody needs to know.'" Mikey said. He was ten.

"He told me that he would help me get a new bike" said Doug

"Larry was going to talk to Miss Peters about my English Final grade" said Kevin

"Promised to help my mom out with the rent one month if I did stuff" added Darren.

Inside the cabin, nobody moved. Outside the cabin, the frogs enjoyed the first warm and clear night of spring. With the temperature in the mid-seventies, it was a perfect Southern night. The yellow flies hadn't come out yet, and the humidity hadn't started to climb. These were the nights that made this camp a favorite for the kids. A raccoon waltzed across the camp compound toward the main hall and the kitchen area. Life was good for the creatures when campers visited Camp Hope. With visitors comes garbage, and garbage is dinner for the raccoons.

Shawn, still standing in the middle of the cabin, looked from friend to brother to another friend. Kevin, his sweet, funny, cute little brother, saw the fury in his eyes as Shawn turned his way, hands on his hips now and his fists in tight balls. Kevin moved over to Jacob's bunk bed and sat partially behind Jacob, feeling safer but unsure about what was happening. Kevin knew Shawn's temper, and even though it's never been directed at him, he's afraid.

"What are you guys saying? Larry is some kind of a freaky pervert?" asked Shawn, truth dawning in his eyes.

"Sounds crazy but it's true," Darren said, barely above a whisper. His hands lay in his lap, his head and shoulders were slumped over like an old man's.

"Darren, you too!" pleads Shawn. "You believe his shit?"

"Shawn, I lived this shit, man," Darren said, looking up into Shawn's eyes first and then at Jacob for conformation.

"Shawn, the guy is pure evil," Johnny said. "Just like we learned in Sunday school." Johnny was a big kid for his age, and sometimes other kids thought him tougher than he was. Johnny was a quiet, gentle giant.

"He lied to all of us," Chris added.

"Good news is that once you get over ten, he leaves ya alone," Johnny said. He had turned ten last August.

Kevin started to cry. He let out a small, hurt-animal whine that grew to out-and-out screaming fury. He turned around in the bed and buried his face in his pillow to keep the rest of the camp from hearing him. Nobody understood whether Kevin was so angry because he now understood that most of his friends had suffered the same thing or because he was only eight, and had two more years before he could get away from Larry.

Kevin jumped up from the bed and kicked his knapsack in the corner of the cabin. Shawn stared at his baby brother as if he was an alien from Jupiter. The kid never lost his temper, even when the boyfriend had beaten him so bad. Kevin kicked the knapsack harder until Keith, his best friend and the same age, got up off his bunk and walked over to Kevin. Without a word, he put his arms around Kevin and pulled him close. Kevin fought for a second, then calmed into Keith's embrace. He'd totally worn himself out. Keith led Kevin over to sit next to Jacob again and sat down beside him with Jacob on the one side and Keith on the other. Kevin was protected by their leader and his best friend, so he calmed down.

"I'll kill the bastard," snarled Shawn. Boyfriend Number Two was responsible for Shawn's colorful language. He worked at the shipyard as a welder, and he used a ton of words neither of the boys had ever heard until he was still living in their house.

Jacob spoke again. "No you won't, Shawn. The reason for me talking about all of this with everybody here is so nobody has to tell about this stuff or deal with this stuff by themselves. Shawn, think about it. If you don't believe us, do you think our moms or Pastor Tim is going to believe us? Guys, if we stick together and all tell our story, then they have to believe us. Our moms will have to believe us. Right? Now if we don't stick together, they'll believe Saint Larry. We need to do this the right way. Together. As a team. One family."

"It's going to be okay, Scooter." Jacob used his nickname for Kevin. Jacob turned around to Kevin and looked down on huge puppy dog eyes. "We're going to fix this guy so he'll never hurt you again. I promise you, little dude, and you know I don't lie."

Jacob turned to the group. Without a word, he met gazes of all seven of his friends in turn. The pain and humiliation of their experiences had united them. They were a brotherhood of suffering. "Okay. Here's what we're going to do."

Shawn had recovered his attitude by now. He was an action guy. Without action, his anger would grow; with a plan, he could control it. "Great, another Jacob plan. We should have known wonder boy would have a plan." Everyone laughed for the first time since dinner. Only three hours had passed, and they'd aged several years in this short period of time.

As the night went on, the raccoon found his treasures in the garbage can outside the back door of the kitchen. Mr. Raccoon ate well on a feast of leftover hamburgers, chips and lots of buns. After he found everything he needed, he wandered back across the compound and into the woods next to the boys' cabin. He would be back in the morning after the garbage from breakfast was put out.

It was almost midnight when the boys had their plan in place and they finally put out the flashlight hanging in the cabin. Most of the boys slept better that night than they had for months. They felt that their plan would be a success and that they were a team. Shawn was the exception—he had all the anger and none of the outlets he needed, so he spent the rest of the night staring at the ceiling and coming up with his own plan to get even with Larry Cunningham.

CHAPTER 6

▼

As Jennifer Kollman walked toward her modest house, she said to herself, "Just a few more steps; just a few more steps. I can make it just a few more steps." In keeping with her normal practice, Jennifer was trying to multitask every minute of her day. She was running late yet again. It was six thirty, and the kids still had not been fed. She'd stopped off at Wal-Mart to get groceries, and it seemed that everyone on the eastern shore of Mobile Bay had decided they, too, had to have hot dogs and buns tonight. The crowd was unbelievable. She had initially tried the self-checkout line, but that didn't work, and then she had taken everything off that line, put it all back in her shopping cart, and unloaded it again at the checkout with a human being.

It had been a typical day with more to do than the nine hours would have allowed. She had actually taken a day off the previous weekend while the kids where out of town and had gone shopping for clothes at the outlet mall in Foley with the girls. She hated to admit that they had all had a great time and had even gone for a drink, a mudslide after the shopping trip. One mudslide turned into three apiece, and she and Jamie had headaches the next day. The kids returned from camp, and there had been a hundred things for her to do, including piles of laundry, so she hadn't gotten to the grocery store until today. The kitchen was out of everything, and the shopping trip had taken longer than she had planned.

Jennifer balanced the three grocery bags on one hip and her overweight purse on the other shoulder as she dug her key out and leaned on the front door. "Why do I put my car keys back in my purse when I know that I'm going to need them to get into the house?" she wondered aloud. She had brought home files from the office tonight to try not to heap more guilt on top of her by spending more hours than absolutely necessary at the office. She had noted that the outside light was already on and hoped that Jacob had already done his homework. She was not in the mood to beg or negotiate with her kid tonight. About the time she got the key out of her purse, the cheap plastic Wal-Mart bags started to break open at the seams. "I only have a few more steps to the kitchen. Please don't break, please hold on for a few more steps," she begged the bags.

Finally getting the key in the door and opening it with a push of her hip, she fell more than walked into the front hallway.

"Jacob!" Jennifer called out, shuffling into the kitchen. The plastic bag split, and a can of French-style green beans barely missed her exposed big toe in her open-toed heels. "Honey, where are you?"

"In the kitchen, Mom," Jacob said just as she rounded the corner and saw not only her son, but also his two best buddies, Shawn and Chris. The boys sat at the table but had no homework in front of them. The TV in the living room, which could be seen from the table, was off. Chris and Shawn looked down at the table top with a "we need to confess" look on their faces.

"Hey guys, who's hungry?" she said as she put the groceries on the counter. "I stopped and got hot dogs, and there are plenty for everyone." With this last statement, Jennifer looked up at the boys. "What's wrong?" She froze mid-step, a bag of buns in one hand and a new mustard bottle in the other. From the looks on their faces, she knew that they were troubled.

Nobody immediately answered, which scared her worse than anything. "Jacob, honey, what's wrong?" She put down the buns and mustard, left the groceries on the counter, and walked toward the kitchen table, looking from face to face, assessing what in the world could cause these serious looks on these young faces.

Jennifer moved into the breakfast area and sat down next to her son at the table. Shawn and Chris looked at Jacob, waiting for something to happen, waiting for him to start. Nobody moved, nobody breathed, nobody blinked.

"Mom, I've … we've got something we need to talk to you about." Jacob said with a huge sigh. "You're not going to believe us; we've already figured that out. But please, no matter what you want to think, you have to promise that you'll listen to everything we have to say before you tell us we're crazy," he begged. "Mom, do I lie? Well, have you ever known me to lie about anything that was important? I know I've made up stuff that wasn't exactly true, but have I ever lied to you about anything major?"

"What's up, baby? You're scaring me. Of course I'll believe you, honey. I've never known you to lie to me; why would you start now? Honey, you're scaring me. Come on, Jacob, out with it." Jennifer laughed. "There's nothing we can't fix."

"Mom, I need for you to say it. I need for you to say that you are going to listen to me and believe what we have to tell ya." Jacob said.

"Ofcourse, honey. I always listen, don't I. I know you don't lie to me, now come on what's up guys?" asked Jennifer.

"Mom," Jacob started, knowing that this was really going to sound crazy. "We need to tell you something about Larry. He's not the guy everyone thinks he is. He's done some things that are really, really bad."

"Yeah, Ms. Kollman," said Shawn, "Larry is not a cool guy. I didn't believe it either, but the guys started talking when we were at camp, and Jacob had already put it together before everyone else admitted what they knew."

"Look, Ms. Kollman. The thing is, we all had classes about this type of stuff last year at school," said Chris. "Well, the third and fourth graders had a class. I guess they thought the first and second graders were too young, but it would have been a good class for them to have with what Larry was doing, even to them. Anyway, it started everyone thinking about what Larry had done."

"Guys, I'm confused. What are you guys trying to tell me? What could Larry have possibly done that would cause all this seriousness?" Jennifer laughed again nervously.

Jacob gave a heavy sigh. "I'm just going to say it, okay? Mom, this is really embarrassing to talk about so just listen okay?" He put his face in his hands. "Mom, Larry has been touching us guys. Do you get what I'm saying? He's been touching boys, kids even younger than us."

"That's right, Ms. Kollman. He even did it to my little brother Kevin," Shawn said and slammed his fist on the table.

"What?" whispered Jennifer. "What do you mean, touching? You mean like, he's hugged you guys? Like he hugs because he is proud of you? Like when you guys won the softball tournament?" Jennifer asked, but in the back of her mind, she knew that was not what the boys meant.

"No mom, not like that. Like the other kind of touching" admitted Jacob.

There were few things that a parent would reject hearing from their children, but when Jennifer heard her child say that he was being abused; her mind immediately rejected the information. The idea that this would happen to her normal child was beyond anything that Jennifer could understand. She thought that she must have not heard the boys correctly. Perhaps she was more tired than she thought and had misinterpreted what they were saying. These were good kids. Larry was a respected member of the church. She had spent time with him on church projects and had sat next to him at baseball games. Nothing like this ever happened in this town, and nothing this freaky ever happened to her.

The boys slowly repeated everything they had told her and gave her examples and times, situations, and details. She listened until the reality of what they were telling her sank into her mind. Then she calmly got up from her small dining table, patting her son on the hand as she walked by him, and went into the kitchen. She leaned over the kitchen sink and threw up.

CHAPTER 7

▼

It took the boys about twenty minutes to tell their story. It took Jennifer only seconds to decide what to do. She first called the boys' parents. Jennifer knew all the moms, and she was very concerned that all of them be involved immediately, so she asked them to come over to her house. Understanding what she had just heard would be harder for some than others. She gave thought to speaking with the parents' one at a time. That just didn't seem quite right, and there seemed to be strength in numbers, or so she hoped.

She still thought the kids had made this up, that it was some kind of joke that they were playing on her and that any minute, they would start to laugh. Jennifer didn't want this to be true. If it were true, what kind of mother had she been to this boy; how could she not have known that this was happening to her son? If anyone other than Jacob had told her about Larry Cunningham, she wouldn't have believed it. But one thing she knew for sure was that Jacob wouldn't lie about this or anything this important. She had started feeling guilty, but her guilt quickly changed to rage.

"I'll kill the bastard for hurting my baby," she thought. But it explained a lot about what had been going on with Jacob lately. She'd been worried for weeks about her son. His grades suffered for the first time since her divorce. She thought that the move to Alabama from Atlanta may have done it, that maybe it was just too much of a shock with all the changes. She felt all the normal guilty parent feelings. "Good grief, I've screwed up my great kid by leaving his low-life father."

There would be tons of time later to commit emotional suicide; right now, she needed to keep her focus on protecting her son and the others. God, what would her ex-husband think when he found out this had happened? She knew that he'd hold her responsible for not protecting Jacob. Hell, she had left Atlanta for just this reason, thinking that crazy stuff never happened to kids in a sweet little community like this. Stuff like this happened in big cities all the time with the drugs and the gangs. They did not happen in Loxley; nothing happened in Loxley. Things like this certainly did not happen in her church. Good lord, help us all.

Hot dogs and dinner were forgotten. Phone calls were made; Jennifer's house became the center of the crisis. All eight kids were brought to the Kollman house, mothers in tow. The kids knew what was coming. The mothers were concerned that Jennifer was okay. She had the miserable job of telling what she knew to these stunned women. Jennifer waited until all the women were present before she told them as much as she could remember about the boys, there discussion at the camp and their decision to bring everything forward hoping that these women, their mothers would know what to do next. They had faith that by all the boys sticking together they had more courage to face whatever happened next to them.

"What do we do now, Jennifer?" asked Jamie, Shawn and Kevin's mother. Jamie was controlling her anger, which was a good start. She always blamed Shawn's anger on his father, but everyone knew that Jamie wasn't completely innocent on that account. She had her own temper, but she kept it in check, only allowing it to overflow when it came to the boys. "I can't imagine that this is true but I also can't believe that the boys would make it up either. Larry has been such a good force in there lives or so I thought."

"I know. I didn't want to believe them either but I must say, once you have heard the details from your sons, you will have no doubt about their honesty. It is true. Larry Cunningham has been sexually abusing our children for years. And right under our noses." Jennifer had been the one that the boys had come to, but she didn't want to make the decision on what to do next by herself. She knew she wasn't prepared for this situation and was scared that Jamie had turned to her like she had an answer. She didn't want to be in charge here. Somebody else needed to take control, and in that moment of her hesitation, somebody else would.

"Wait one minute," said Chris's mother, Kim. "Let's think this through completely." She stood and moved to the center of the room, physically taking command. "These boys have already been through a lot. I can't even believe that we're all here having to deal with this. I feel bad, terrible, in fact, for all of us. These babies, my God, what have they been through? This is a disaster, and I could kill Larry with my bare hands right now if he was here." She sighed. "But let's think about what this is going to do to these kids. They've already been through so much, having this done to them, deciding to stand up for themselves, having to plan and come to Jennifer tonight. We can't undo everything that's happened before this moment. But we can control what happens next to these boys, our children. If we go to the authorities, everyone will know what's happened. Everyone in the church, everyone in the school system, maybe even the newspaper, for God's sake. It could be on the news. I know that they can't publish our names but people will figure it out. Don't you think they will figure out who we are? Do we really want these kids to be publicly embarrassed by this? I mean, really, what will people think?"

The room instantly went silent; the women heard crickets outside through the open window. Nobody moved; nobody so much as took a breath. It was well known that Kim was all about appearances. The daughter of a doctor in Mobile, Kim had learned early that appearance was everything. She had been publicly embarrassed when her husband died in a plane crash. He was supposed to be on his way to Honduras with Doctors without Borders to assist in surgery for disadvantaged children. When his plane went down over Vale, Colorado, with his twenty-year-old secretary but no medical gear on board, Kim had tried to make up for her humiliation by buying a new house and a new BMW, coloring her hair Clairol number 104 blond, and buying a new wardrobe of short skirts and tight tank tops that were way too young for her. Kim looked good but felt bad. She hadn't done well as the merry widow; she was too embarrassed to enjoy spending all the cheating bastard's money. "I think that perhaps there is another way to handle this. Maybe something a little more direct and a little quieter," she suggested.

"Kim, this is not about perception or appearances," whispered Jennifer, trying to get the conversation back on the right track "This is about protecting our kids from a damn pervert." Jennifer had actually given thought already to some way of covering up what they knew, but she didn't want to admit that in front of everyone. What if they just told the boys to keep quiet? What if they moved to another town, maybe Daphne? What if she told Jamie's second cousin, Bubby, about this mess, and he just beat Larry Cunningham to a pulp and then they got the kids to a good therapist? She couldn't work it out in her head, so she had rejected the idea.

"I can't believe you're so shallow, Kim," said Jamie, always the first to say whatever came to her mind without much thought about how she said it. "You're worried about what people think of *you* at a time like this? Your son has been through hell, and he deserves justice. Forget what people are going to think. Protect these kids and all the other kids in town." Jamie had grown up a little more hippy than the rest of the women. She had also been taught to fight the injustice in the world even though the injustices of the world seemed to visit her a little more often than she thought she deserved.

The boys, who were still in the room, got up and moved toward the stairs to leave. They had sat through the story again, and a couple of their mothers had wanted verbal confirmation from them that what Jennifer had said was accurate. But this was what the boys had feared: that their mothers wouldn't support them. They had talked about the fact that they were kids and that grown-ups never believed kids. In a subconscious show of brotherhood and support, the boys needed to be closer together, so they moved away from their mothers and into their own group. A couple of the mothers had a problem letting go of their hands when they walked away. The boys physically came together as a group at the base of the stairs, looking across the room at their mothers.

Kim moved over to the window and stood with her back to the room, not daring to look at the boys or her friends. She had been through a lot, and this seemed like it was just too much to handle. Chris moved away from the group of boys, stepped behind his mom, and hugged her around her waist. She turned away from the dark window where she couldn't see anything and looked at her son. There were tears in her eyes even before she looked down at Chris.

"Mom, it's going to be okay. I love you. We'll get through this together just like we do everything else. I promise," Chris said with much more maturity than anyone had seen from him before. "Do the right thing! How many times have you told us that? No matter what the cost, do the right thing. Mom, this is the right thing."

"How did you get to be so brave when your mom is such a chicken?" she asked with a laugh. Kim hugged her son tightly, as if someone might pull him away from her any minute and she'd never lay eyes on him again.

"Good genes, I guess." Chris laughed and headed for the stairs and his friends. He stopped at the bottom of the stairs, grabbed his little brother around the neck in a choke hold, and pulled him playfully up the stairs, leading all the other boys.

As the boys disappeared, the mothers had a minute to collect themselves. One thing they had learned as single mothers was that not doing anything got you nowhere. Standing still was something that single parents didn't have the time to do and couldn't afford to do. Jennifer and the others knew that they needed to move to keep from going crazy. The rest of the discussion was short and sweet. Jennifer was elected as the spokesperson for the group. It was agreed that she would contact a friend's ex-husband who worked for the Baldwin County Sheriff's Department and file a formal report the next day.

The group also felt that Tim Cunningham, their minister and Larry's brother, should be contacted along with the police. Jamie volunteered for this task. She had been through a lot with her kids and had a great relationship with Tim. The pastor had worked with her to keep herself together and to be stronger for the kids. She had spent hours in discussions with him about how she could work to find the peace that she needed to raise these boys. Everyone believed that Tim could help in this situation. They understood that he was Larry's brother, but he seemed to be able to put things in the right perspective in any situation. Their minister was a fair and decent man regardless of what his brother was.

By the time the group reached consensus, it was past midnight. The boys had been back from camp for less than forty-eight hours, and everyone was exhausted. The boys all stayed the night at Jacob's and slept on the floor. It was strange how they all felt safer together than separated in their own houses.

The mothers decided that Darren's mom, who was a nurse, would get information about physical exams for the boys who had been abused and get the name of a really good counselor for all of them, even the ones who hadn't been touched by Larry. One for all and all for one.

"We should all consider some type of counseling at this point. I know I'm going to have some deep discussion with Dr. Wilson about this shit." Jamie had been seeing a counselor for several months, trying to put her life back together and to understand where the anger she felt every day was coming from.

Mikey's mom worked for an attorney in town as a research clerk, and she offered to get the name of a good lawyer who handled children's issues. They all agreed that if they couldn't just hunt Larry down and kill him, they would see him rot in jail. "I should be able to have this information tomorrow, and when we get back together, we can review qualifications and talk about the costs of legal counsel."

Johnny's mom, who was a teacher at the high school, committed to call the boys' school counselor, let him know what the situation was, and get any advice he had on dealing with it. "This is going to be in the papers. I don't think that they can publish the boys' names, but you know the word is going to get out. What if other parents don't want our boys around their kids because of this? My God, what is my ex going to say about this?"

They had all thought the same thing. They had all invited Larry into their homes. They had all flirted with the guy, openly making a play for him at one time or another. All of them had done it, some more blatantly than others, but they had all done it. Now, they were embarrassed by their actions, and they were angry at what he had done.

Everyone had a job that would help channel all the hurt and anger into a constructive place. Jennifer would act as the coordinator for all the information. They agreed to stay in touch and work through whatever happened together. They would be there for the hard conversations and the finger-pointing from their ex-spouses. The boys were a great example of how they needed to pull together as adults. The boys had done a very brave thing, bringing this information out in the open, and the adults now had to do their part.

"You know, those little men have more guts than we do." Kim said.

More than once during the discussion, someone talked about getting even. Jamie volunteered, "Cutting his dick off would be a good start." These were women who had dealt with bad men in their past. They were friends, they loved their kids, and they were mad as hell. Kim said, "If we could just get rid of him quietly, the boys wouldn't have to go through the embarrassment of answering all the police's questions." They all wished that something could be done to just make this situation and the next steps go away. Mikey's mom said for sure that her ex-husband would shoot Larry's ass off when he found out.

"Forget all this," said Jamie, "Let's just make a couple of phone calls, and this guy can be knocked off for about five hundred dollars."

"Do they call it knocking someone off?" laughed Kim. "Actually, it's not a bad idea. It would make everything go away, and we could be done with this thing. Hey, I've got the money if someone had the contacts."

"Hell, I know some good ol' boys from up the road in Stapleton that would take care of him for nothing," Johnny's mom said. "My ex would probably be glad to do it. He has no problem shooting those damn deer every year; why would a little blond bastard like Larry slow him down?"

"You guys are not funny, and we need to stop. Stay focused. Let's call Wes and get the police involved before this goes too far," Jennifer stated with as much authority as she could muster, knowing that she would love to see somebody beat Larry within an inch of his life.

"I don't know. If we call the police and he goes to jail, how long will he be in? A year, maybe two?" asked Kim. "That's not enough!"

"What if they don't believe the boys? I mean, it's a bunch of kids against an adult, a pretty high-profile guy for this small town. It's Larry, y'all. We were all fooled by him. What if everyone else is fooled by him, too?" said Mikey's mom. "Don't you think people will think the kids just got pissed about curfew or something and turned on him?"

"Damn y'all, I've been trying to go out with that guy for two years, and now I find out he's had sex with my eight-year-old son," Jamie said. "I think I'm going to be sick. What are we going to do? Our babies, my God!" Jamie grabbed her own hair like she was going to pull it out.

"Hold on, everyone. The main thing right now is that we don't lose it," Jennifer said very quietly, looking toward the stairs as if wondering if the boys could hear them. "The boys hung together as a family, a team. We have to be as brave as they were and hang together, too. Please, let's not freak out. We have to do this right! We need to trust the system. I know that sounds corny but it is the only way to get beyond this thing."

Jamie was standing next to Jennifer, and Jennifer reached out to take her hand. They had been through a lot, and Jennifer understood that Jamie was the most volatile of the group. She also knew that Jamie, when she needed to, was capable of getting very aggressive for her sons. Kim walked to Jennifer's other side and took Jennifer's other hand. All the ladies got up and, just like a Girl Scout promise ceremony, they all joined hands.

"All for one and all that stuff," Jamie said.

At a little after one o'clock in the morning, the single moms from the Loxley Luthern Church held hand and held each other mentally together, but they knew that it was just the beginning.

CHAPTER 8

▼

When you live in a small town like Loxley, you never think about whom you know and what they do for a living until you need their special talent. Jennifer knew that she needed to get help from someone in law enforcement. This was bigger than anything she knew how to deal with herself. So she fell back on who she knew, and she had known Wes Harmon for years. Jennifer had grown up in Loxley and after College at the University of South Alabama, she had moved to Atlanta where the money was better and the opportunities for a young graduate were greater. Before she moved to Atlanta, she had been friends with Wes and his ex-wife. She had run into him around town regularly since she and Jacob had returned to the area, not socially but in the grocery store or in at the school park during baseball games. He was known to be a fair guy and someone that was connected throughout the state of Alabama in law enforcement. She had no choice really, he was the only member of law enforcement that she knew, so he was a good starting place.

When she called Wes the next morning, he agreed that he would come over that afternoon around six to speak with her. She gave him the advance notice that this was a disturbing legal matter that she didn't want to talk to anyone about until she had spoken with him. Wes wasn't overly concerned by Jennifer being vague about her situation; this happened to him a lot. It was generally something like a missing dog or a neighbor who someone was thought to be selling drugs. Maybe it was a dispute over a fence line or a kid with a noisy radio; he didn't know but wasn't really concerned.

All the kids stayed with Jennifer the night before and stayed home from school that day. The mothers had agreed to meet back at Jennifer's house that afternoon to discuss the situation with Wes. They started the ball rolling with their assignments, and all the women had a much better focus on the situation by the time Wes showed up at Jennifer's house.

"Okay, let me see if I understand," Wes said after he had listened to their story several times. He started by having the mothers tell the story. Then, the boys were all brought into the room, and they were asked to repeat the story for the police officer. Jacob took the lead again and started the story with what they had all agreed to say the previous night. Wes listened with a great deal of patience, not stopping the kids until they were finished and had all had an opportunity to add bits of information. Wes was an experienced interviewer and asked the right questions a number of different ways to make sure that the story from the kids didn't change with each telling.

After the story was complete, Wes suggested the kids go upstairs and wait while he spoke with their moms. "So, what I understand is, your kids all went to Camp Hope for the weekend, and they came up with this story that one of the most respected guys in town has been sexually abusing them for a couple of years." He had been very patient and understanding. "Are you all sure that something else didn't bring this on? Maybe Larry pissed off the boys at camp, and they decided to just show him and cooked this story up in their heads?"

"I knew this was a bad idea," Kim said, the first one to cave on her convictions. "I told you guys that we never wanted the attention that this was going to get. He's a cop, and he doesn't even believe us. We should just deal with this dirty little secret ourselves. Take the kids out of the church, don't let that monster anywhere around them, and maybe move them into a different school." She stood and moved over to the window again.

"What the hell is out that damn window?" Jamie asked. "Kim, no, we are not running from this. I'm not raising my kids to run from a fight against a monster. Is that the way you want to raise your boys to react when something bad happens to them? Let somebody hurt, abuse, *screw* with you and roll over and take more? Or worse, hope that they just leave you alone and go after your best friend next time? Is that what you want your kids to learn by hiding this 'dirty little secret'? I'll kill Larry before I'll let him get away with messing with my boys."

"I've sure that won't be necessary, Jamie," Wes said with a sigh. "Let me talk to the boys for a minute. You know, man to man, so to speak." Wes had been in law enforcement and around women enough to know that about half of what parents say about their kids was rooted in the parent's over protectiveness. Wes also knew that kids tell stories. A lot of stories. Heaven knows his four had told their share.

"Not a good idea," says Kim. "If you're talking to my kid, I'm going to be there." She didn't turn from the window as she spoke. Jennifer could tell that all Kim wanted to do was be out of there and not in this house having this conversation.

"Kim, just let Wes handle this," Jennifer pleaded. Jennifer was the only one in the group that could get along with Kim and make her understand what was right. Jennifer crossed the room to Kim and patted her on the arm. At the touch, Kim's shoulders loosened up, and she seemed to relax just a bit.

"Just give me a few minutes," said Wes, moving toward the stairs. "Let me talk to the guys, and we'll be right back down." He disappeared upstairs, and the ladies all heard a light knock on Jacob's bedroom door. The door opened with a squeak and closed again with a soft click.

Jennifer got up to put on more coffee. Jamie got on her cell phone to call her boys' father. The conversation had to be done, but she wasn't looking forward to it. Kim, Darren's mom, and Chris's mom wandered out the back door to sneak a cigarette while they had a chance.

An hour later, everyone heard the boys' sneakers coming back down the stairs. Wes brought up the rear of the group with his arm around Jacob's shoulder.

"Let's go, Mom," Shawn called out as he reached the bottom of the stairs. The boys weren't smiling, but they looked relieved. The smaller boys just walked directly to the front door as if nothing had happened, and it was just time to go home.

"Whoa, boss," Jamie said. "What's up?"

The women all stood, moving like a protective bunch of geese over their goslings when danger was near.

"Wes says that we should all go home. It's late and we have school tomorrow," Chris said, as if it was just another day.

"That's right, ladies. I have the basics from the boys, so now you ladies need to take the boys home. We'll all meet back together tomorrow to get more information," replied Wes. "Just make sure that you guys don't talk with anybody else until we get back together."

Wes told them that the sheriff's department had a special division to handle child abuse cases, and they should all come to the station after school and bring the boys, and he'd have all the appropriate folks together to take their official statements. "This is not my specialty, ladies, and I'm in a little over my head here. The boys sound like they really believe what they're saying, but I just don't know enough about molestation to ask the right questions. Listen, just work with me here. Let's get the pros working on this tomorrow."

"You mean you believe them? You believe their story?" asked Chris's mom. There was obvious relief in her voice and face. His belief in the boys somehow made it all better.

The officer and the boys moved to the front door. Wes opened the door and held it for them to pass through. As Wes stood in the yellow light of the front porch, he looked down at the brown sheriff's hat in his hand. He fingered the brim of the hat and considered the questions for several seconds. He moved to the edge of the front steps and took one step down before looking out at the cars holding those tender little lives that had been forever changed by what they believed was fact. Wes stopped and turned back to their mothers. "No way these kids could have made that stuff up. They had too much detail, and the younger ones gave me graphic descriptions of what happened. They're too young to have seen it on TV or understand what they were saying if wasn't true. Off the record, I think the bastard is guilty as hell. We'll see what we can prove."

The ladies all started to cry. Jennifer cried from relief at having someone else taking control of this situation. Jamie cried from anger and confusion, not knowing what the "stuff" that Wes was referring to might be. Kim cried for the embarrassment of it all. The other mothers cried from the stress and fear of not knowing what was going to happen.

CHAPTER 9

▼

Meanwhile, I was struggling to connect with Cora, my seventeen-year-old foster daughter. Cora and I were sitting in my livingroom with the TV on and dinner in our laps.

"Honey, why were you yelling at Joe last night on the phone?" I asked Cora, who was shoveling ramen noodles into her mouth. This was her favorite dinner, and the kid only weighed a hundred and five pounds and was five foot seven. I didn't understand how anyone could eat that stuff every day and not gain an ounce. She was a beautiful girl with the long, lean body of a model. She had long, sandy-colored hair that lightened up in the summer with her perfect tan.

"Because he is so stupid sometimes," was her answer between bits of creamy chicken-flavored noodles. She chased the noodles with Dr Pepper, which she drank by the gallon daily. I was mentally counting the carbs in this dinner and trying to remember the last time I saw her eat anything green. She and I would need to have another discussion about her diet, but this day was not the day, not while she was in a bad mood from fighting with her boyfriend. If I ate that stuff every day, I'd weigh four hundred pounds, have three chins, and thighs the size of watermelons. I'd be on the six o'clock news when the firefighters had to cut me out of my front door after I had a heart attack and died.

Cora had lived with me for two years. She was seventeen years old and knew way too much to be so young. She was like most foster kids and had seen things that I couldn't even rationalize within my normal perspective of the world. When she came to me she had already graduated from drug rehab at fifteen years old. We talked endlessly about what had happened in her life. She had been sexually abused by family members early and it had left her jumpy and distrustful of all males.

The girl hadn't had a break since being born to two people who were more concerned about drugs than their baby girl. Once, we were watching a show on TV, and she pointed out the mistakes that the script writers had made in their presentation of how to cook crystal meth. Fifteen years old and she knew how to cook crystal meth. There were so many things wrong with her situation that all I could do was love her as much as possible and try to make her life better. The fact that we had gotten to the point of worrying about her diet and not her drug addiction was a huge indication that she had turned her life around. Concern over a teenagers diet was so much easier than concern over her drug addiction.

She was a beautiful kid but needed a lot of direction and even more love. I tried my hardest to keep her safe and make her understand that I valued her. She hadn't always trusted me, and after this much time, she still thought that the smallest thing would get her sent away to the detention center in Baldwin County or to another foster home. I spent a great deal of time making sure that she received compliments every day. My friends and family all worried that I would spoil her. I could only hope that would be possible. I didn't think anyone who hadn't had positive reinforcement or a single kind word for fifteen years could be spoiled after only two years of love and attention.

She and I tried to spend what we both called "normal time." We did little things together that she had never done with her mother, like cooking meals and shopping for clothes. We had our nails done together. I reviewed her homework and talked to her teachers, like a parent should do, to monitor her progress. Cora and I spent a considerable amount of time talking about her future. We had hundreds of discussions about the consequences of her actions and the need for her to react to events in constructive ways.

Cora's father had been sent to jail several years ago, and her mom had walked out when she was four years old. She started getting into trouble when everyone seemed to have deserted her. She, like most foster kids, was moved around for several years, giving her no stability and no direction. She was housed, but that was it. The best she had felt about herself was when she had finished the rehab program. She came to me as a last resort, or so the social worker said. They had tried everything they could think of, but she could not be moved into a foster home with other children because she had issues with other children, actually her wanted to beat up all other kids, even the boys. For the last year and a half, she had been making good grades and going to school. We had our trials—she skipped school and got mouthy with teachers—but we have managed to make it through all that. Cora had a temper, and we were trying to learn how to handle that mouth. She hadn't hit anybody in more than a year, and that by itself was a victory.

"What did Stupid do now?" I asked moving into the kitchen to brew iced tea. I got "the look." "The look" was the one that parents got when they did something that proved they didn't have a clue. Like when her friends were over and I asked "who is M&M?" I got the look and was told that his name was Eminem. Or when I made the mistake of asking what she thought of my new jeans, I got the look. Why didn't she date the cute guy who bagged the groceries at Winn Dixie? The look. I got it a lot. I'd learned to have fun with the look and sometimes, when I was feeling frisky, I would say something just so I could get the look. It started with a major eye roll. I wondered if anyone ever researched the look to see if the eye rolling could cause future damage to her developing brain. My guess was that they hadn't done the research, but that for every eye roll a teenager did, their children's eye rolls increased threefold. Cora's beautiful face made the eye rolls even funnier, and I loved watching this kid's reactions to me, whether they were intentional or not.

I deserved this particular look on this day because the first rule for boyfriends (and husbands, for that matter) was that you can say anything about your own, but parents were not allowed to say a word about them. Calling Joe "Stupid" was okay for Cora but was way out of bounds for me. I knew that in her seventeen-year-old way that Joe was the love of her life. I knew I shouldn't have said anything, but I did it anyway just for the fun of it. I smirked a little as I said it.

One of Cora's former foster families had lived in Joe's neighborhood. They had met like any other kids in the neighborhood. Joe had taken an instant liking to this beautiful girl, and they started to date. He was a couple of years older than Cora, and he had no idea how streetwise she was. There was no way that he could keep up with her.

The good news was that to give me the look, she had to actually look away from the TV and *SpongeBob*. Teenagers could have complete conversations for years on end while staring at the TV. It was amazing that she recognized me at all in public because she didn't look at me half the time we were talking. We were both huge *SpongeBob* and *South Park* fans. Every Wednesday night, when the latest *South Park* was on, we watched it together. We loved *SpongeBob* because he was so good, and *South Park* because the kids were so evil. These were the normal things that we did together, and she thought it was okay. This was about where my coolness ended and my momness began. I had learned that I could only partially let myself be her friend. It was hard enough to supervise a child this troubled who wasn't yours. If I wanted to win a popularity contest, it wouldn't have worked for either of us. She needed direction and guidance more than she needed friendship.

Even though she was not technically my child, I was the closest thing that she had to a mom her whole life. Since her dad had been sent to jail, she like many other foster children had been moved from relative's homes to foster homes to group homes. She had never stayed anywhere for very long. The fact that she was with me after more than a year gave me the greatest feeling of accomplishment. I felt that I was doing something worthwhile. It was this that made me know that regardless of the look, I was, on some level, getting through to this child.

"Cora," I said from the kitchen, "tell me why you were yelling at Joe. What in the world could he have done?"

"Joe is jealous of everybody, including my girlfriends," she said through the noodles again. She waited for a commercial to give me this small amount of information about the current fight.

"He thinks that if I'm with my girlfriends that he needs to know exactly where we are and what we are doing." Joe had been the boyfriend du jour for six months this time. This was the second try with Joe; they had broken up for about sixty days two months ago, and it almost killed all three of us. Cora was miserable because he was her boyfriend and her best friend. He was miserable because, God bless his soul, he loved the girl. I was miserable because when Cora was not happy, I was not happy.

Boy, I would have loved to explain to her first that Joe was still a kid; second, that Joe was twenty but still living at home with his mother and not working steady; and last, that Cora was much smarter than Joe, and he understood that. Instead, I said, "Really, and what do you say to that?"

I had struck a nerve. That question got me a full face response. Cora actually turned away from the noodles and the TV and looked at me. If there was one thing that this kid wanted, it was for someone to listen to her. She would do anything to get my attention, and once she got it, she could demonstrate the full drama of her seventeen years. Then she was a happy camper. I knew that I was about to get the full force of it as she faced me to get her point across.

"I told him that the only reason that he has a problem with my friends is that he has issues." She gave me an eye roll. "I told him that he's too controlling, and he needs to learn to trust me" Finger pointed for emphasis. "I told him that relationships never work without total trust." Arms across the chest. "I told him that he must be feeling guilty about something that he's done and that he is projecting his guilt on me." She stood up, pushing out her right hip at a remarkable angle.

Skinny and bony as those hips were, I thought they might just bust through the too-tight, too-low-cut jeans. How did she make these long statements without taking a breath between sentences? She picked up the bowl of noodles and shoved another forkful in her mouth as she walked toward the kitchen.

"Honey maybe he is just worried about you." I knew at that moment that she had been watching too much Dr. Phil.

"That is so not the point. Regardless of what has happened in the past, if we are going to move forward as a couple, he needs to trust my judgement." She moved into the kitchen putting her dish away in the dishwasher.

"Well I am sure that tomorrow will be another day and you two will work it out." I say in my best non-commital Human Resource Manager way.

SpongeBob and Patrick were getting in trouble because Patrick got caught blowing spit balls at SpongeBob in Undersea School. The squid teacher saw Patrick but missed what SpongeBob did to earn the spit ball to the head, so only Patrick got in trouble. I could never compete with that. I gave up and called, "Taking a bath and going to bed. See you in the morning, love!" She moved back in front of the TV and I was forgotten.

No response needed, none given. I left the living room and went into my bedroom.

"Oh, by the way," I said sticking my head back out the bedroom door. "I'll be in Bay Minette tomorrow. I have jury duty. If you need anything, call my mom or call my cell. If it's an emergency, call my mom. She can get to you faster than I can." You would think I was talking to a much younger kid, but Cora was a little, ah, high maintenance. She got in a lot of trouble years ago but had been a good kid for the past several months, but she was still a little needy.

"I'm not a child, you know." she said just loud enough for me to hear. I couldn't see her, but I knew she used an eye roll again. I could tell from the tone of voice. It's so interesting that when she needed something, she quickly played the "I'm just a kid" card. But when she didn't want to do something, she was an adult all of a sudden. And I'm an idiot.

"Whatever!" I answered and snickered to myself. I loved to use the whatever answer. It drove me crazy when she used it on me, so any chance I got to do it to her was fun.

Before she came into my life, I had never laughed so much or cried so hard. She was a blessing, in a masochist kind of way, she filled my need to protect and defend someone. She filled my need to nurture and develop myself and another human being. Here was a kid who had no idea who or what I was two years ago, but we had become closer to me than she was with most of her blood relatives.

She was getting very close to the magic age of eighteen, when she would be allowed to get out of the foster system, and I was growing more concerned about her ability to maintain her sobriety on her own every day without some sort of supervisor.

I was scared for her and concern about the decisions she would make. She had no foundation for making the decisions that she would need to make in her senior year of high school. One day she was going to the local junior college; the next day it was the navy; and the day after that, she was getting married to Stupid Joe. The married to Stupid Joe idea seemed to be coming up more often lately. We were only a couple months away from graduation, and I couldn't count how many conversations we had that ended with both of us hugging and crying, worried to death about what the following months would bring.

She was the hardest thing I had ever done, but the best thing I had ever done. I loved this kid like she was my own. And often, I felt that locking her in a closet until she was thirty would be safer than letting her free. I justified these thoughts with the idea that it was for her own good. It may be the same whether you're a biological parent or foster parent.

As I climbed into the tub of very hot water, I wondered what I would have done if I didn't have this kid in my life. Being a foster parent was harder than anyone would ever admit. If the social workers did admit now difficult being a foster parent was to prospective foster parents, no one would ever take these kids into their homes. Some people said it's harder than being a real parent because you have only a few months or, if you're lucky, a few years to undo everything that had been done to these kids for their entire lives. You had no relationship authority like the real parent—you had to earn any respect that you may get. With the younger kids, you lived every day thinking that their parents are going to come and take them back. With the older kids, you spent every day scared that they were going to run away or do something to get in more trouble than you could get them out of. I loved this kid and felt horrible that I couldn't take the hundreds of Baldwin County foster kids into my house to love. I felt that this was my only way of taking care of children.

My ability to take care of children's issues would change shortly.

*   *   *   *

At seven that night, Officer Wes Harmon was still at the office preparing for what would be an interesting day tomorrow. He had just finished the reports from the child advocate about the Lutheran kids, as they are now being called around the station. Wes closed the file and pushed it to the far side of his old, metal desk, which had three drawers and a broken front leg. The thing wobbled without the leg, but it was his desk and had been for many years. This old desk and his job were both predictable and consistent while everything else in his life was being turned upside down. At least he got a comfortable new chair a couple of years ago.

Wes sat with his face in his hands, still picturing what happened to those kids. The report from child advocacy was very detailed. It was amazing what they got those kids to tell them, using interview techniques designed specifically for children. "I've got to get a new job," he said to nobody since he was the only person in the station house at this hour. Everybody except two dispatchers went home an hour ago.

The report was written with quotes from the children that would be used later in court. Somehow it seemed sadder to read the report of sexual abuse in the words of a child. Adults could filter what was said; children didn't have the ability to express their thoughts through filters so you got the true horror of the misconduct through their eyes. An innocent that doesn't use the standard words that we all hear and read in music, movies, books; the description of sodomy sounds even worse from the mouth of a child.

Wes Harmon was a father himself, and he couldn't understand how anyone could do this to children who were as young as seven years old. Wes had dealt with some sick people in his past but he had been lucky that he had never had to deal with a child molester before. What would he have done if something like this had happened to his own kids? He had no idea, but he could guarantee it wouldn't be pretty.

All the victims were from single parents, and that hit way too close to home. Wes's wife had left him, and he'd lost many nights sleep wondering what affect their bad decision were going to have on his kids long-term. Wes had been a better father than he had been a husband. He loved his kids and enjoyed spending time with them. It was the ex-wives that he hadn't enjoyed. They hadn't been anymore happy with him than he was with them. Women had a way of learning to hate him after the very heated lustful phase of a new relationship. He had never been able to maintain that lustful phase through the realties that were a normal relationship. The realities of his work and the stress that having to deal with criminals put on him and therefore on their relationship, where the reasons he said that he had the ex-wifes.

Wes knew that he had to do something other than stay at this desk; he had to go home. He hated what going home meant. It meant being alone, and he did not like being alone. Going home to the silences, the ghost of what his life was like when he had his wife and kids with him in his house was the worst part of every day. All his co-workers and his captain thought that Wes was driven and that he lived for the job because he spent so much time working nights and weekends. The other cops on the force told him they believed that he was the most dedicated cop they had ever met. Truth be told, he had learned to hate the job. He knew that he had lost most of these relationships to two things: his job and his drinking. The reality was that Wes was tired of the paperwork, tired of the thankless job, and sick and tired of the courts having more respect for the criminals than the people defending the public. Everything about this job was old and tired and made him sick. He hated this life but couldn't see a way out of it.

He knew the numbers. He understood how many times the legal system failed to do what it needed to do. He had been involved so many times with situations where law enforcement lacked enough evidence or proof to get what they needed on a criminal. He also knew that there were dozens of examples where the work paid off and the criminals had gone to jail only to be let out on reduced sentences that hardly seemed fair for the crimes they had committed. He and his co-workers sat at the bars several nights a week drinking away the disappointment of the failures in the legal system. He'd lost a huge case five years ago when evidence had been misplaced, and the drug dealer had walked out of the courtroom right in front of him smiling and waving over his shoulder.

Wes got up from the desk and grabbed his jacket from the back of his chair, he needed to get out of there and get his head straight. He looked one more time at the Lutheran kids' file and tapped the top of the file with his knuckle, hoping that tomorrow would turn around his run of bad luck.

CHAPTER 10

▼

If you've ever been through any management training classes, you know what personality type you are. I, Katie Race, was a driver, or a type A personality. I was a planner, a task-oriented person who believed in having goals and working with a plan. Results mattered to me, and given a room full of people, I would try my best to organize the entire group, regardless of the situation. This type of personality meant that if I got a subpoena to jury duty at 8:30 a.m., I would arrive at the Baldwin County Circuit Court room at 8:15. I'm not anal, I'm driven. There is a difference.

I walked into the courthouse and saw a number of people that I'd known my entire life. Such was life in a small town in lower Alabama. The line to get through the front door was long, and the hold-up was the new regulations to have everyone pass through a metal detector before they were allowed into the courthouse. These regulations had started just after 9/11, and I was amazed that we even did this in Baldwin County, Alabama. What terrorist would want to blow up the Baldwin County Courthouse? I guessed that it was more about crazy people fighting over custody or divorce settlements in Baldwin County than it was about terrorist. "Nothing ever happens here," I thought and smiled. Two weeks later I would remember having that thought that nothing ever happened in Baldwin County and laugh at how naive I was before that day.

My purse was searched, and the most incriminating thing they found was a copy of Tim Dorsey's *Stingray Shuffle*. Dorsey was funny but not politically correct for an HR manager. Screw it; I liked the underbelly of humor. *South Park*, Carl Hiaasen, old *Saturday Night Live*, that kind of thing, which explains a great deal about me. Since receiving the subpoena, I'd spent a lot of time planning what books I would bring with me. I'd heard from everyone who ever served on jury duty that you spent hours just sitting, waiting for something to happen. I thought I was in heaven: no employees to talk to me, no drama to get drug into. I was really looking forward to the time away from work, away from needy employees.

I made my way to the front of the courtroom, a cup of Joe Muggs coffee in one hand and my book in the other. My purse was hung over my shoulder. If I had to be here, I might as well be front and center for the show, so I moved towards the front of the courtroom and sat in the front row. Joining me in this overly air-conditioned room were 250 other good citizens of Baldwin County. "Good," I thought, "what are the chances that I'll get picked for anything? They have tons of other choices for jurors." I felt good that I was out of work and ready to read my book.

My plan was to have a free week from work to read Dorsey. I could read anywhere, so these lawyer types wouldn't distract me from my purpose. My first thought after getting to my seat was how uncomfortable the seats were. The seats were made of hard wood and shaped like church pews. Damn, not a good reading environment; I'd find a better chair to stake out. I eyed the judge's chair up in front of the courtroom. "Bet his chair is nice and comfy," I thought. "I wonder if anybody would notice if I just pulled the judge's chair down here." The seats for the general schmucks like me were rock hard and we were packed in tight, sitting was meant to keep you wide awake and feeling guilty about something. Just like church.

I settled in to the pomp and circumstance of bowing at the foot of justice as the judges, the district attorneys, and support staff entered the room. I watched as they all entered the courtroom, chest held high, proud of themselves. Judge Jim Black was a first-rate guy who had been in office for fourteen years. He was one year away from his retirement, and I'd heard that he couldn't wait to serve his time and get out with his pension from the state. Judge Black had run honest and open campaigns through all of his elections. He didn't play dirty, and he didn't mess around in the courtroom. He had a reputation for getting things done and not allowing the lawyers to get off track. He gave us a little overly prepared speech about our duty as Jurors. I could tell from his speech that he enjoyed the attention of being in front of the potential jurors and that he must have given this speech many times over his years in office.

Outside the office, Jim Black had been a good friend of my parents' for years. I got a wink as he recognized me and settled his long black robes over the arms of his comfortable chair. I shifted my weight on the wooden pew and tried to remember that I was serving justice here and supporting freedom of the American way of life. Damn these pews were hard. "Hmm," I thought, looking over at the judge. "Last time I saw Jim, he was drinking rum and pineapple juice out of a hurricane glass with more fruit in it than Mom's ambrosia salad at Thanksgiving." I smiled and settled in for a two-week mini vacation in this courtroom, book in hand.

He continued his speech about our duty as jurors. "These are hard but important times in our world. We have troops, some of your children, overseas fighting and dying for your right to be here for the next two weeks. They are defending with their lives your right to sit here and review the crimes put before you. This is your chance to do your small part in upholding the justice system." Judge Black spoke with all the polish of a practiced politician. I was actually a little moved to believe that what I was doing here was a privilege of our justice system and I part of me hoped that I would get to service on just one jury to be able to see how the process worked. I was under no illusion that I would be picked, there were so many of us here.

I actually put my book down and listened. I looked around the courtroom. He had our attention; nobody said a word or moved a muscle. I had come in here thinking that this was a chance to hide from real work for a week, but as Judge Black continued with his speech, I believed that I may have had something to offer here. He told us that we were part of a great process, one that changed lives and served up justice to those who, without our honest consideration, might go unpunished and might hurt others again. At the same time, we were here to protect a way of life that kept the basic fabric of a controlled society in balance. Without the justice system we would have chaos.

I was moved and kept my seat; my book was folded in my lap, my eyes on the man I thought I knew for drinking boat drinks at our beach house. Call me crazy, but I actually believed what the judge was saying. I believed that this was my chance to make a difference in my community. Judge Black let the current attendees know that he and the court understood that there might be certain circumstances that limited even the most loyal of patriot's ability to serve at this time and he gave the jurors presence the ability to approach him with any concerns they might have about serving at this time. With this the flood gates opened and a rush of people moved to the center aisle to speak to the judge. Approximately eighty-five other "good citizens" were not moved to protect the American way and got in line to bargain with Judge Black to let them forego their duty to the court system. They believed that even though the American way of life might be at risk, and even hanging in the balance, they needed to be selling used cars at the Toyota dealership in Daphne and not sitting on a jury. Let someone else uphold the American way of life; they need to make money. I was surprised that so many people had missed the point of the Judges speech.

After showing an amazing amount of patience with these pathetic excuses, Judge Black again called the potential jurors to order. It was now ten fifteen, and the judge had released everyone he planned to excuse on that day. He asked for our attention, and those poor souls who couldn't lie well enough to get out of the room quietly sat down and listened. Our numbers were much smaller now and I grew more concerned that my plan to finish an entire book might be at risk.

"Okay, down to business," said the judge. "The first step in the process is to select what is called a grand jury. We will select eighteen people from the remaining available jurors to serve for two weeks. Being selected for grand jury is an honor and a privilege and is not to be taken lightly. The purpose of the grand jury is to establish a filtering system for the cases that come through the district attorney's office, and eventually, to these courts. Over the next two weeks, these good citizens will represent the general population in important decisions about what charges will be brought before the five judges in Baldwin County. I will be drawing names from the remaining potential jurors for this duty. I will ask the following individuals to please make your way to the front of the courtroom and into the jury box when your name is called." With the assistance of the clerk of the court, he started the selection.

The names of the jurors condemned to the grand jury were randomly selected from the remaining jury population by Circuit Court Clerk's computer. The names were printed on small scraps of paper and given to the judge to read. When he got to number five, he called my name.

"Well, shit!" came out of my mouth. I had a problem with the control valve that kept everything in my head from coming out of my mouth. I'd been known to claim that I have Tourette's syndrome, but no one's bought it. It was more a redneck thing than a medical condition. I tried daily to tighten down on this valve and keep my thoughts to myself. Luckily, I didn't say this very loud, and only a few people knew what I actually said and laughed at me, but not with me.

Judge Black looked over his glasses as if he had made a mistake by calling my name and seemed to wonder if I would be a troublemaker. I waved at the judge, hell I've known this guy and his wife for years. Judge Black had known me and my parents all of my adult life, and my inability to keep my mouth shut was no secret to him or anyone else who had known me for more than fifteen minutes. It was a problem I had, or "an opportunity," if you're a human resources manager. I needed to work on it.

As I worked my way over to the jury box, stepping over and on several people's toes as I went, I dumped my lukewarm coffee on Dr. Miller, my dentist, and dropped my book at the end of the bench when Mr. Nielsen grabbed my ass. I swore it was on purpose, even though he immediately apologized and said he was trying to help. I spoke to family friends, police officers, and court personnel that I knew.

Once all eighteen of us were in place in slightly more comfortable chairs in the jury box, Judge Black told us to stay put and let the other jurors have a break to move their cars away from the courthouse. Parking on the courthouse square was limited to two hours, and we had been there two and a half already. The local cops would give you a ticket even if you were there to uphold the American justice system that they defend. Even the Bay Minette police department needed to keep the money coming in. Heaven knows there was nothing else to draw people to this one ring circus of a town; they had to take advantage of jury week. While everyone else got to smoke a cigarette and move their cars to parking lots off court house square, we squirmed as the DA and his assistants looked us over like we were lunch specials at the Downtown Carriage House.

As the last of the regular jurors left the courtroom, Judge Black turned to us for more direction. "As stated in *United States v. Cox*, the grand jury is both a sword and a shield of justice—a sword because it is the terror of criminals, a shield because it is the protection of the innocent against the unjust prosecution," stated Black, as if he were reading from the holy grail of justice. We were given another prepared speech about the purpose of a grand jury, the need to keep everything confidential, and the role that our new best friends in the district attorney's office would play over the next two weeks.

Before he dismissed us, Judge Black chose the foreman of the grand jury. There was a tradition behind this process in Baldwin County. Judge Black explained that more than forty years ago, Baldwin County had an attorney who always wore a wool hound's tooth hat on days he came to court. It became the tradition that when the decision to name the Foreman of the Grand Jury was to be made all the slips of paper with the Jurors name on them were placed in his hat and a random drawing determined the foreman. When the attorney passed away, his widow willed his hat to the Baldwin County court system. To this day the same hat is used every time a Foreman of the Grand Jury is chosen by this random draw.

The famous hat was presented to Judge Black by the sheriff, who was required to witness this process by law. The court clerk added the jurors' names to the hat, and Judge Black quickly reached in to draw a name. We all held our breaths waiting for the name to be read. Judge Black told us that the foreman had additional responsibilities to the Grand Jury. The foreman was required to keep the records with the DA's office and to sign all the records at the end of the two weeks to certify that the indictments were correctly recorded. I did not want this additional responsibility, it sould like to much. When the name was drawn, Mr. Fedewa was named the foreman of the jury.

"Thank God," I said and received another look from the judge. "Tourette's!" I tried to explain, which got a laugh from the judge and the rest of the jury. They were happy they weren't chosen either.

I didn't get a laugh from anybody sitting at the DA's table. They were a serious group of people, and I was instantly scared of them all.

With the preliminaries completed we were all told that we would be escorted to the Grand Jurors chambers. Following our foreman and the bailiff, we filed out the back door of the courtroom and into the hallway. We walked down one flight of stairs, which were unlocked by the bailiff and locked behind us by a second bailiff. I started to feel a little special, if not confident, by the process. The grand jury was guarded, and we had our own stairway. How cool was that?

We found out later that the bailiff was the guy who got things if you needed something. He made sure that we had cookies and chips, Cokes and coffee. He could also get us through the security gate at the front door faster in the mornings if we were nice and smiled really sweet at him. He was our new best buddy. He also was not bad looking, which was what I thought as I followed him down the hall when we were moved down the back hallway. For some reason, brown polyester looked good on him. Hmm, must be the size of his gun I thought.

We followed our bailiff down two flights of stairs and through the door marked "Grand Jury." The chairs here were even more comfortable than the ones in the main courtroom. We quickly found out the reason for the comfortable chairs was that our butts would be welded to them for the next two weeks. There was not a chair made that would be comfortable after sitting in it for two weeks.

The grand jury room was set up like a jury box in a very large walk-in closet. It had three rows of seats. It was smaller than my kitchen, and we had eighteen jurors, two people from the district attorney's office, and witnesses in this room. Each row contained eight seats; more than we needed for eighteen of us, which did allow us to spread out a little. In the front of the room were two Wal-Mart folding tables laid end to end and a chair for the foreman, one chair for the witness, and two for the DA's representatives. The juror's seats were in three rows in cinema style with the third row being the highest and the first row only six inches off the regular floor. The drab walls were covered with pictures of the last twelve

Baldwin County sheriffs. None of the pictures were hung straight, and over the next two weeks, different jurors would get up from their seats and straighten them.

Our grand jury was made up of fourteen women and four men, all from various walks of life. We had one mail carrier, two insurance salesmen, one schoolteacher, one banker, one social worker, four retirees, two college students, one engineer, three stay-at-home moms, one newspaper reporter, and me. While everyone got comfortable, we introduced ourselves, shaking hands and polite smiles. Over the next two weeks, we would learn tons about each person's life, both during lunch breaks and during our deliberation. The first thing we learned was that our foreman, Fedewa, was hard of hearing. He had neglected to tell the Judge about this when he asked if there was any reason that he could not serve as foreman. This slowed the process over several days and required patience on our part as we repeated several points and he missed much of the testimony which had to be repeated for him. We started out on the first day thinking that his condition was mildly cute, and we felt for him. By the end of the first week, we all raised our voices to near screams to try to help him out and get the process moving quicker.

Three very properly dressed people stood at the front of the room. The two I knew were David Whitman, Baldwin County district attorney, and Judy Hooks, assistant district attorney. They were watching us like we were zoo animals behind glass, trying to assess who were where and what we were thinking.

David was an intense fellow whose motivation in life was getting in front of the TV cameras so he would be re-elected. David had been DA in this county for as long as anyone could remember and would be in that role as long as he was breathing. Unlike most lawyers, David was also an Academy Award–winning actor. Well, not really, but he had spent a lot of time in front of the camera and providing entertainment in the courtroom. His stage was the courtroom, and the local six o'clock news cameramen would jokingly whispered, "and *action!*" when he got up in front of a courtroom. David knew the exact time that the local papers began to roll presses, and he used this knowledge to make sure that they never delayed waiting on a quote from him. He never missed handling a big case or meeting the grand jury personally.

You would hate David if you met him outside the legal system, except for one thing. He appeared arrogant, egotistical, and self-important, but David was the best at what he did. The guy knew his way around the courtroom and was able to work a jury with the drama he caused. He did the drama better than anyone else, winning more cases than anyone. And for that reason alone, the citizens of Baldwin County continue to re-elect him year after year. The citizens forgave his being a dramatic actor because the show was worth the drama.

Judy Hooks, probably a better attorney than her boss, was the perfect second-in-command. She was funny, charming, and exceptionally bright. She knew all of her boss's jokes and laughed on cue at each one. I wondered if she sat at home at night plotting ways to get David to retire early, or how to kill him off without getting caught. I wondered if the knowledge that he had no intention of retiring caused her to drink straight vodka shots.

Being the perfect number two, she allowed David to put on his show for us while she stood quietly in the background. David again told us now important we were and that if we needed anything, Judy was the one to ask. David left the room in a hurry because he saw a News Ten van pull up outside through the window over the backs of our heads. We were the first grand jury Baldwin County had sat in a while, and there were a lot of important cases on the docket that we didn't know about yet. David wanted to make sure that the news crew was appropriately briefed to watch the next two weeks, because David was confident that important indictments were about to be processed.

At this point, Judy took the floor and continued with the administrative end of the grand jury orientation. She introduced Matt, a junior assistant district attorney. Matt, who was twenty-four but looked fifteen, bore a remarkable resemblance to Harry Potter—he had the same glasses and haircut. As my mind wondered I daydreamed that Matt would get elected judge someday and laughed to myself that he would really look like Harry Potter with a black robe. He assured us that he did complete law school at the University of Alabama but that we were his first grand jury. Judy let us know that he wouldn't be flying completely solo, and that she was there to back him up if he needed her. With a little bit of cooperation, he was sure that we would "get through it together."

The jurors settled in and when everyone was comfortable, we were given our first case by Harry Potter. Theft of property, first degree. In south Baldwin County, the resort community of Gulf Shores, Alabama had a population of thirty thousand during the winter, and three hundred thousand from Memorial Day to Labor Day. With the transition, from the types of people on the island and the amount of people on the island came a number of problems and minor criminal activity. The houses were sometimes left for long periods of time without any occupants after Labor Day, and those unattended houses became targets. The infrastructure of police and fire had not grown quickly enough to keep up with the increase in the summer population so the homeowners in the resort community were easy marks for the criminals. Such was the case we reviewed.

The first case was two males and one female who entered a beach house during the off season and removed a fifty-two-inch big-screen TV worth forty-five hundred dollars. It was important that we understood the house was on stilts, and the only way in or out, was a wooden staircase that led to a front door twenty feet off the ground. Many beach houses were built this way, not because of the water tides because they are far enough off the water for the tide changes not to be the problem but because of hurricanes, when the tidal surge was another matter all together. This crazy trio of criminals carried this heavy TV down a floor and a half from the house to the ground, and put the TV in the back of a pickup truck. This community is all on an island, so they drove off island to the larger community of Pensacola. They took the stolen property to a pawn shop, which had a surveillance camera, just across the Alabama state line in Florida and walked in to sell the merchandise. The three criminals showed their real drivers licenses and the stolen TV to the pawn dealer. They unloaded the stolen TV from their personal vehicle, from which the dealer took their license plate number. When they completed the paperwork, they used their real names again. The TV was reported stolen, the pawn dealer looked back in his paperwork, and the criminal's real names and addresses were right there in the paperwork. These three all admitted to what they had done and were quickly arrested.

The grand jury members all got a good laugh, and we learned how the process worked. We heard the summary from Matt, then a police officer would come in to add any details that may be interesting or answer any questions, we had minimal discussion about the facts, and asked any questions we needed to have clarified, and then we voted. Easy enough. We all settled into our chairs, some got another cup of free coffee and said, "This isn't so bad" or "that was easy."

Needless to say, we indicted these idiots without much discussion. We laughed how stupid those folks were to use their own license and their own names. I was feeling much more comfortable. "This isn't that hard," I thought.

The next case we heard was theft of property in the second degree. Young men were working on a house in Robertsdale, doing some minor repairs to the roof after a hurricane. They were on the roof for several days in the hot sun making the repairs and looking around at the other houses near by. During that time they noticed that the neighbor behind the house they were working on had a Big Green Egg Cooker on his back porch. I suppose that the would-be thieves thought about how good their cooking could be if only they had a Big Green Egg. The Big Green Egg cookers were very popular at the time and were expensive by grill standards, but these criminals had placed a value on the grill and they decided they needed it.

On the last day they worked at that location, they hatched a plan to steal the Big Green Egg cooker. After they got paid for the roof job, they drove around the corner and loaded up the neighbor's cooker in their truck. They got away with the theft and, on the way home, remembered that they needed to cash their paychecks for the weekend. They went to the bank and used the drive-through teller to cash their paychecks. Again, the criminals were caught on camera, with the Big Green Egg in the back of their pickup truck; the license number was easily visible on the banks surveillance system. The bank gave the videotape to the police, and the criminals had no way to deny that they indeed stole the cooker. Plus, the bank had their names and addresses because they cashed their paychecks every Friday afternoon.

By lunchtime, we were in the groove. The routine was: an officer came in, told us a little about the crime, a little about the criminal and if the loser had confessed. We were amazed at how often people confessed to driving under the influence or making crystal meth. Once we heard all the evidence, we looked around the room to see if anybody had questions, then we voted to send it to the courts or back to the police officer. We joked that we need a new category of felony—stupid.

What we didn't know at lunch on that first day was that Matt was seasoned enough, or coached enough, to understand the general dynamics of a grand jury. Rule number one: give them the easy stuff first. He had loaded the first day up with easy cases that included confessions. This slowly eased the uneducated juror into thinking that stupid felons confess, and you were just there to confirm those easy confessions and send everything to the court for a trial. It was as if he was chumming the water for the sharks that he knew he would train to do his killing. Our job was to listen to stupid felon stories and bless them with an indictment. We were all thinking, "Nothing to it."

Rule number two: progressively give the jurors harder cases once they become complacent about handing down indictments. After hearing story after story the jurors just want to make a decision and move on. The job of the DA's assistant became much easier.

For days we listened to felony DUI after felony DUI story. We learned that some of these defendants had ten or twelve DUIs before they had a felony charge. In Alabama, you must have three "certified" DUIs before you had a felony charge. Unfortunately, none of the law enforcement computer systems communicated with each other, so if you were slightly smarter than the average stupid felon, you drove drunk in Florida or Mississippi and Alabama would never know about it.

If you separated your drunk driving between counties and states, you could drive drunk for years without ever being put in jail for any length of time. We also found out that if the local government officials didn't keep good records, which most of them didn't until they got computer systems, and they couldn't produce a hard copy of the DUI, then the earlier charges couldn't be certified. We were amazed that anyone ever got to the felony DUI stage. I swore more than once during this little education process that I would never drive again. If there were that many drunks out there on the roads with multiple drunk driving charges, I'd be staying home from now on. The lesson learned was, if you got a DUI in the south end of the county, start drinking in the north end of the county. You'd stay out of jail for a lot longer.

When we were sick to death of these, Matt gave us a little meatier topic: unlawful possession of a controlled substance (UPCS) and unlawful distribution of controlled substances (UDCS). These were the fun little cases where I was educated about the rampant use of drugs by my neighbors. After a couple of days of these, the grand jurors could explain how to cook crystal meth and where to buy the components for the mix. There were tons of these cases. The criminals ranged from children sixteen years old to grandmothers who were third-generation drug dealers in the county. It was scary what we learned on jury duty.

On the fifth day, Friday, another domino was put into place by the hand of fate and my life changed. We had heard approximately three hundred cases, dozens of drug and DUI cases, and were getting so comfortable with the process that Matt made the comment, "By next Friday, you guys will be indicting ham sandwiches."

He was right; we had seen and heard enough to know that what our little community looked like to us just five days ago was not a reality. My beautiful little community was full of drunk, stoned, evil thieves who went home to beat their significant others with bats, beer bottles or their bare fist. I had been living next to crazy people with problems I couldn't understand all my life. The only drug users I knew, other than Cora, were on TV. Everything I thought that I knew about the community I had grown up in was wrong. Felons seemed to be everywhere.

It was as if you went to the doctor for a little checkup and he told you that you were going to need major surgery to remove a major organ. You felt fine; you were just going along with your daily grind and, all the sudden, you were dying. My beautiful south Alabama community was rotten and cancerous to the core. We the jurors were jaded and pissed when we got a new deviant category from the felony menu—sex crimes.

Matt was great with explaining the different crimes and the degrees for each: rape, sexual abuse, sodomy, etc. Not only did we get the definitions of each of the sexual crimes, we also got an overall discussion of what it means when people have unwelcome sex with mentally defective or mentally incapacitated individuals.

We reviewed the definitions of rape in the first degree, commonly referred to as forcible rape. It was also engaging in sex when one person was sixteen years or older, and engages in sexual intercourse with a female who was less than twelve years old.

We learn that rape in the second degree was "age rape." This was when the rapist was sixteen years old or older, and engaged in sexual intercourse with a female less than sixteen years old but more than twelve years old, or he engaged in sexual intercourse with a female who was incapable of consent by reason of being mentally defective.

We then covered sodomy (first and second degree), and sexual misconduct. The next category of sexual abuse we were introduced to was when a person was subjected to sexual contact by forcible compulsion or to a person who was incapable of consent. This was generally due to age. I was amazed that some of the things people did to other people sexually were just misdemeanors and not felonies.

We were stunned and confused. We were good people from normal backgrounds. Most of the things we heard that day we may have seen or heard in movies or books, but never in the detail that we heard in that formal, sterile room by a guy who looked too sweet and innocent to even be discussing these situations. Harry Potter should not have been presenting these issues to us. It felt wrong. It felt dirtier than any porn movie ever produced. I felt sick that these things happened here and all I could think was, "These perverts need to be put away for life."

Regardless of how we all felt the hits just kept on coming as we heard case after case of sexual depravity. We hear story after sick story of the deviants in our community. It was the eighth case that really made us mad. It had been a long day of sickening stories about people I wouldn't cross the street to pour water on if I saw they were on fire. Then we were introduced to Larry Cunningham and the Lutheran church kids.

Larry Cunningham, we were told, was a forty-two-year-old white male. He was an unmarried youth minister at the Loxley Lutheran Church, which was just down the road from where I lived. This was my community. Larry's perversion was little boys. We heard the story of how a group of boys between the ages of eight and eleven had recently attended a weekend church camp outing, and when they came home, they told their mothers that they had been abused sexually—some of them multiple times and some of them over a period of years—by their youth minister.

The assistant DA took his time with this case; he brought in an expert to explain how they interviewed the boys and got the details of what had happened. As we listened to the details of what these young boys, these babies had been through, my heart was breaking. I thought about some of the conversations that I had with Cora and knew that some of the same issues affecting these boys affected her also. The woman who handled sexual abuse investigations for Baldwin County came in to speak with us and gave us a great deal of background information, not only on this case, but on similar cases throughout the county. Her name was Susan and from all appearances, she looked quite normal. I couldn't believe that she didn't have nightmares every night of her life, seeing and hearing the stories she heard every day.

"How did Larry Cunningham come to the attention of the county?" asked Matt casually from his folding chair at the card table. The room had grown very quiet, and I'm not sure that anyone was even breathing at that point. We weren't laughing anymore. All the jokes had stopped, and we sat frozen, staring at Matt, then Susan, then back to Matt. We were transfixed as if we were watching the final match at the U.S. Open.

"We were contacted by a group of parents from the Loxley Lutheran Church, who had information about the abuse that had taken place over several years by an individual named Larry Cunningham," Susan told us evenly, without emotion. Susan was tall for a female, six foot easy. She wore a light pink suit with a white silk blouse. The hem of her skirt and the cut of her suit were conservative. I felt comfortable with her instantly and believed that she must make the kids feel the same way. She had a pleasant smile and a soft voice. Her gestures were reserved, and her manner was professional but not emotional.

"And did you investigate these claims?" asked the assistant DA. I am surprised that he also seemed to have no emotional interest in this case.

"Yes," Susan said. She didn't look at us, she looked straight at Matt. She appeared confident in her review of the material, and it seemed like she was discussing her need to stop by the dry cleaners, and not lives of these children.

"Can you recap for the grand jury what your investigation found?" Matt said, leading the witness to tell her story. Matt relaxed back into his chair, understanding that Susan was very good at this part of the process, and he would just be an interruption if he spoke.

"We interviewed the boys, one at a time. They were interviewed by separate social workers who are trained in dealing with children who have been through these types of experiences. The way it generally works is that we ask a series of questions. Depending on how the kids answer, we are led to ask other questions. During the interviews of these kids, they separately identify that Mr. Cunningham had touched them on their genitals. They also identified that he used his genitals to touch their genitals. Here, I have pictures," she added.

My heart stopped in my chest. "Dear God, don't make us look at pictures," I thought but they were not real pictures.

"The kids have communication issues due to their ages and are asked to visually communicate what happened" Susan said.

She dug in her briefcase and produced a group of sad little drawings that started out as stick figures printed on the page. The children were asked to draw a circle around the parts of their bodies that had been touched inappropriately. All the pictures had the genital area circled by the kids. They were then asked to draw an arrow to the part of the adult stick figure, Larry's body that he touched them with. All the pictures had an arrow drawn to Larry's genitals.

At its most basic level, it was a way for these children to tell their stories with the minimum amount of details. This was understandable because they were too young to be able to communicate what happened in adult terms. Too young to understand what had happened to them except they knew that they were hurt and that it was wrong.

I had heard the stories of how several of the foster children that I'd come in contact with had suffered similar horrors, but it seemed farther away than this. I had seen the faces of these kids and knew the effect that their abusers, the sick bastards, had on the rest of their lives. I would never be able to understand why anyone would do these things to children, but I knew the effects never went away. Kids never did "get over it." They did not "grow out of it." People always say that they'll forget, that they were so young that the pain faded with time. Bullshit. It never went away, they never stopped thinking that it might happen again and yes, I knew that it affected their soul. I had seen this with Cora, and I knew it to be true for other foster children I had spent time with. No amount of punishment could equal what this man had done to these children.

I'd heard the stories from my Department of Children's Services worker about the amount of sexual child abuse that went on in our county. I had talked to my "girls" about what had happened to them, but never in this kind of detail. I had three girls in addition to Cora and their babies, and had spent a great deal of time talking and listening to their stories. Cora and I talked about the abuse that she had seen and been exposed to at an early age. She had only been ten when the sexual abuse started, and it had been horrible by anyone's standards. We cried and hugged and talked for hours about how you get beyond it and learn to live a different life. She had never shared the details of what happened; she only told me who had done things to her, and that her parents had known that the abuse was going on but were too stoned to do anything to make it stop. But these kids were seven and eight years old. They were babies.

It took us only fifteen minutes of hearing the tale of this trusted and respected man who was sexually abusing young boys in his church to decide his fate. If he had walked into the grand jury room at that moment, several of us would have physically attacked him.

At the time, I had no idea the affect that this little bit of information had on me. Shocked, angry, repulsed, we understood that we were here to make a difference and get this sick guy away from children. All the things that Judge Black and the district attorney had presented to us that first day made sense now. We felt that what we were doing was important. We understood that, yes indeed, we had a duty to serve here. We had been given the responsibility to get this guy off the streets, no matter who he was, how much money he had, or what he could pay to get himself out of this. I was truly proud to be there for those eight young boys and only prayed that their young lives could be salvaged with a minimum amount of damage that had already occurred.

"Let's take a break," Matt suggested after we had voted to indict Larry Cunningham. "I think we need one and it's about time, anyway." We all moved for the exit door at the same time. Nobody spoke to each other; we were all too deep in our own thoughts to talk. Perhaps it would have been better if somebody would have brought up football or what Brittany Spears was up to, but nobody did. The moment stayed heavy and we allowed it to fester for awhile inside us.

When we returned from our break, we moved on to other felonious stupidity charges. Most of us wouldn't give much thought to Larry Cunningham until it was reported in the paper that Larry was going to a sentencing trial.

*   *   *   *

Lindsey, one of the members of the grand jury, sat at the Bay Minette Country Club later that same night. She was sipping on a martini with three olives and thinking about her day. The Country Club was a small place with a private bar. There was nothing going on this Friday night: no golf tournaments, no bingo, none of the usual celebrations like a wedding or an anniversary, and the only reason this member of the grand jury was in this bar was because she had taken the day's events to heart. Lindsey was a newspaper reporter; the information from today would have made excellent material for her paper.

Lindsey understood that what she had learned today about all the cases must be kept confidential. She also understood that she had taken an oath to keep that information to herself, and not to discuss it with anyone. Lindsey had graduated from a fairly good journalism school two years before and she had looked for a job with a top-flight newspaper. She had sent out hundreds of resumes and gone on twenty job interviews. The only offer she had gotten was from the *Mobile Press Register* working in the Baldwin County section. She was stationed in the Bay Minette location which was not even the main office. They were treated like step-children and not given many of the opportunities for promotion that the Mobile associates were given. Her dreams had quickly faded. She tried to tell herself that this was just a starting place, something bigger and better would come along. Heaven knew she needed something better and soon. The student loans were getting the best of her, and she was barely making it on her menial salary.

All she needed was one really big article that would start her career, she had told her mother. She needed that one lead that put her in a position to write an article that would be picked up by the national press, and then her career would be off and running.

She had heard such a story today when the grand jury indicted Larry Cunningham. Nobody had the story yet. She had insider knowledge giving to the Grand Juror that the trail jurors would probably never hear. She had covered a number of cases with the court reporter and understood that, in many cases, the actual jury didn't get all the best information, and the grand jury was given a lot more leeway with documentation. There was only the DAs representatives there and they gave information to the Grand Jury with no one present to object. Often, the attorneys were successful in keeping information away from the courtroom that the grand jurors were able to have. Lindsey had all the details of the case and she knew that the story was a good one.

As she sipped on her martini, she thought that if she could get a story in the paper prior to the other newspapers, she could have a real crack at getting the first front page article. She was sure that this kind of a case would have front page, national coverage and she needed to be the one to get her byline on that article first. If she was careful and published the article the day they went to court then it would look like she had just gotten the information from the court records. What were the chances that something that she had seen in the grand jury case wasn't going to make it to the trial? What were the chances that she would get caught?

And what exactly would the judge do to her if she did get caught using confidential information for her article in the newspaper?

She finished off her seven-dollar martini and did something she could ill afford—ordered another. She decided that the drink was worth it, and the risk of using everything that she had learned was also worth the risk. She would make the information look like good reporting, and there wouldn't be any problem, right?

She called to the bartender. "Can I get one more of these delicious martinis, honey?" And with that order, her plan was hatched to give life to her dying career.

CHAPTER 11

▼

There was a knock at Larry Cunningham's front door; he looked down at his watch. It was eight thirty on a Tuesday night, a strange time for someone to knock on his door without calling ahead of time. Larry turned off the computer where he has been surfing the internet for children's games for church and walked toward the front door.

Larry was dressed casually in jeans and a "God Rocks" T-shirt. He didn't have shoes on, but his toenails were nicely manicured, as were his fingernails. He turned on the living room overhead light as he walked through the front hallway. His house was not a large one, and it was old; most of the floors were original white pine and had been polished to perfection. Larry kept a neat and orderly house. He didn't have a lot of visitors, but when his brother or one of the kids stopped by, he liked everything to be clean and in place.

"Just a minute," Larry called with a questioning voice, not knowing who it might be at his front door. Larry looked in the mirror on the wall beside the front door to check his appearance before he checked the peephole for who it might be. Then Larry realized that he had not turned on the outside light and couldn't see a thing outside. As Larry stepped back from the door, he turned on the porch light. He checked the peephole again, and saw Jody Alegrie, chief of police, and one of Jody's junior officers.

His first thought was that something must have happened to one of his kids from the church. Maybe one of the kids had gotten mad and run away from home. This had happened before, and the parents always thought the kids may have gone to Larry's house.

All the church kids knew Larry's house, and because he wasn't too far from town, sometimes older kids would drop the young runaways at Larry's. They had all visited many times for cookouts, youth group Christmas parties, and even sleepovers for the boy's birthdays. Larry loved his kids and would do anything for them, including providing temporary reprieve from angry parents. Larry always called the parents as soon as the kids were occupied with something else, so no one would worry.

Larry recognized Jody; they actually had gone to church together for awhile before Larry's brother had gotten his own church. Larry felt duty bound to join Tim in his new church. Larry was very happy with the church because there were more kids, and Larry was all about the kids. They were the future of any church and the most innocent of followers of Jesus.

"Hey, Jody, long time no see, my friend," Larry said, opening the door with his biggest brightest good ol' boy grin.

The younger officer, who looked vaguely familiar to Larry, immediately grabbed his arm, pulling him out onto the porch.

"You have the right to remain silent, Asshole, and I suggest you try just that," said the officer as he turned Larry into the wall of the house just a little too roughly. Larry hit the brick siding just a little too hard and woofed out a breath of air.

"Hey, wait just a minute" said Larry very surprised.

"Take it easy, son," said the chief calmly. It took a lot to get Jody upset; he had seen rookies like this get overexcited a lot of times. The best way to deal with them was to calm them down.

"No need to get yourself in trouble unless he wants to resist arrest. You don't want to resist arrest, do you, Larry? I think the kid here would really enjoy it if you did." The chief leaned casually on the railing on the front porch, letting the younger man grab and shove Larry into the bricks on the side of the house again. The young officer was making a point, and the chief wasn't sure that he didn't want to do the same thing to this bastard.

"What is this about, Jody?" Larry was confused, trying to get his face off the bricks and turn to look at the chief who was smiling oddly at the blood running down Larry's face.

"Now Larry, I have a hard time believing that you are the least bit surprised that we are here." Jody smirked. "Go ahead and read this poor excuse for a human being his rights, son and try to do it the right way, so we don't have to let him go tomorrow morning because some yellow-dog Democrat judge lets him go on a technicality."

"Jody, wait, what is going on here? You know me, Jody, I wouldn't do anything illegal" Larry said.

The younger officer still had Larry's face pinned to the brick wall of the house, a forearm across his shoulders. As the officer began reading Larry's rights again, the chief turned to look over his shoulder into the dark front yard. He heard a grunt from Larry as the young officer drove his knee into Larry's lower back and pushed his face harder into the wall.

"Take it easy kid, you don't want to mess up that pretty little sissy face, do ya? He's going to need his good looks where he's going. That face is going to make him real popular." The chief walked down the front steps and onto the grass below. "Okay boys, y'all search the house and the property and see what we can find." The chief called into the darkness of the front yard. With that, several officers stepped out of the darkness and moved toward the house. "Make sure you check the bedrooms. Bet they're pink and frilly if I had to guess."

"Wait a minute," said Larry "What's going on here, Jody? I'm serious; what are you guys doing here?" There was the beginning of the sound of panic in his voice.

"Good," Jody thought. "This guy needs to be out of his comfort zone; it will make the confession easier to get."

"Well, Betty Boop, you've been indicted by the grand jury for the state of Alabama on twenty-two counts of everything from sodomy of a seven-year-old to sexual abuse of several little boys in your church. Life as you know it is over, my revolting friend." Jody gave him the news with a little smile and a slap on the shoulder. He looked at his hand as he removed it from Larry's shoulder and involuntarily wiped his hand on his pant leg as if he had touched something slimy.

"Yeah, and one of those little boys is my third cousin, you disgusting pervert," said the officer who had been holding him against the wall. He turned Larry a little harder than necessary and pushed him, handcuffed, off the porch, toward the police cruiser.

"No police brutality, son. Let's keep this clean until the boys at the big house in Atmore get a hold of this pretty little girl. They really love child molesters, Larry. You're going to be very popular, very popular indeed as pretty as you are. Should be some fun nights for ya over the next ten years," the chief said, sneering at this obnoxious piece of crap he once called a friend.

"Jody, I have no idea what you are talking about. I haven't done anything." Larry called just as he was pushed into the back seat of the police car.

Jody watched as Larry was loaded into the cruiser. Just as the door to the back seat is closed, one of the officers from inside the house stuck his head out of Larry's front door.

"Jody, you got a minute?" called the officer, breaking Jody's musing. Jody and his wife had talked several times about the overall affect that the job was having on Jody. It was times like these that Jody thought long and hard about when he was planning to retire. He had told everyone that it would only be another year or two until he was free from the county job; then his wife had decided they needed a bigger house. Damn if he would ever be able to get away from these foul late-night discussions with horrible, immoral monsters like Larry Cunningham at this rate.

"Yea, I'll be right there," Jody said as he moved towards the front door.

CHAPTER 12

▼

It seemed like a good morning in south Alabama. I walked into Joe Muggs for my morning worship at the altar of the coffee gods. Terry was behind the counter this morning, and she looked up as I entered the door. She was the best server Joe Muggs had working for them; she was the one I saw almost every morning when I worked next door. It was still early and she wasn't finished setting up for business, but when she saw me coming she immediately picked up a cup.

"Hey, Katie," she called out, grabbing the tall latte cup off the shelf. She knew what I liked and was reaching for the sweet brew before I got it out of my mouth

"Mornin', Terry," I grumbled as best I could at this hour on a Saturday morning. I hated working Saturdays, but when we have new hire orientation, it's the only day that I can get everybody in and completed in one day. "Sugar Daddy latte."

"Tall, right?" she asked, knowing the answer before I shook my head yes. Joe Muggs is a chain but the flavored coffees are heaven. My Joe Muggs was inside a Barnes and Noble bookstore, which made it even better because they would let you take a book off the shelf and read it while you drank your coffee. They knew if they could get you reading you'll have to take the book home.

"Tall is fine, unless you have it in an IV bag to go, yes?" I answered. I placed my arm right across the counter as if she were going to put on a strap and pull the needle out from under the cash register.

"With you in two seconds," she said, picking up her pace and moving faster once she got a good look at me. "How's the Orange Box today?" she asked. She had worked in retail long enough to know that big box retail is a wicked game.

"Too early to tell, my dear, too early to tell," I said as I moved over to the free newspapers. I could tell I was one of the first customers because the paper was still together in one piece. The advantage to getting there early was that I could actually find all the paper. If you were an hour later, customers have taken parts they want to work with them and only a partial carcass of the paper was left. I'm in here every day, so I know the drill.

The headline stopped me in my tracks. "Youth Minister Arrested for Sexual Abuse." All the sudden, I was completely awake. I scanned the first paragraph and confirmed that Larry Cunningham had been arrested.

"All right!" I screamed in the middle of Joe Muggs. Terry looked up at me. "Sorry," I apologized to an older couple who came in after me and were sitting at a little table next to the Bestseller Rack.

"My coffee's not that good, Katie." She laughed, placing the top on my heaven in a cup.

"Of course it's that good, but no, it's not the coffee." I held up the paper. "This jerk was arrested." I showed her the article on the front page. "I was on the grand jury that indicted him and now they picked him up. Real sleaze ball, you should read this." I handed the paper over the counter to Terry. She took a look at the front page and put in to the side for later.

"Oh yeah, I saw that article this morning. Guy sounds like a total pervert. How can he do that to children? That guy should be shot." Terry worked on the coffee for the older couple who had actually purchased a paper and were reading the same article.

"No kidding. Pervert is the nicest thing anybody will call him for a while," I called, picking up my coffee and toasting Terry over my shoulder "Thanks Terry, have a great day." I have a new bounce in my step and a coffee in my hand "This is going to be a great day," I said to a mostly empty parking lot.

*   *   *   *

At the same time, twenty miles away, Jennifer, Jacob's mom ran down her driveway in her bare feet to get the paper. She wore lounge shorts and a sleeveless T-shirt with not much else. She hoped none of her neighbors would see her make her morning dash for the paper. She hadn't brushed her hair or taken a shower, so being seen would not be good.

As Jennifer picked up the paper from the driveway, she looked up in the sky. The morning sky was a little dark for this time of day and it looked like rain again. When she got back in the front door, she pulled the paper out of the plastic wrapper and put it flat on the counter in the kitchen. Before she could turn to start the coffee, she noticed the headline.

"Youth minister arrested for sexual abuse," Jennifer stopped with the coffee pot frozen in midair in her hand. She quickly read the article; all the facts were there in black and white. Larry Cunningham, youth minister, choir director, fire-fighter, abused church's children for years in a small community church in Baldwin County. The article also stated that a U.S. Department of Justice study had shown that nationwide there were between 103,000 and 149,500 substantiated sexual abuse cases a year, between 1990 and 1998.

> *Larry Cunningham was arrested at his home and is being held by the Baldwin County Sheriff's Department until his bond hearing, scheduled for Monday.*

Jennifer read the article three times before she put the coffee pot back into the coffee maker and turned it on. The article was not encouraging. It gave three other examples of men who had recently been convicted in Mobile for sexually abusing their own children. The article pointed out that it often took years to bring the sex offender to trial and get them in jail. In one such case, the father was molesting his daughter, and the police were required to use the daughter in a phone call to corner the man by having his daughter talk to him on the telephone and ask him why he had hurt her. Jennifer breathed, "Oh my God," as it hit her for the first time what the boys would be required to say and do to get Larry in jail. The article pointed out that victims who didn't reveal the abuse for a long time, who hid the memories of the abuse for many years, made it harder to recreate the events because there usually was no longer any physical evidence. It was still possible to get convictions, but it made it more difficult.

"Physical evidence? Oh my God." The reality was overwhelming to Jennifer.

Events could trigger a child's memories, the article alleged, and compelled them to remember and report the abuse long after the specific events. It stated that in one case, a TV program sparked a family discussion between a sister and brother when the older brother made fun of the rape of the girl on the program. His sister then told him in detail about an aunt's boyfriend who had raped her at age ten.

The sister, now sixteen years old, and her family were staying with the aunt at the time. The boyfriend told the girl that he would kill her and her whole family if she told anyone. The girl and her brother went to their mother, explained what had happened, and the ex-boyfriend was arrested. However, because the abuse had occurred years earlier, the defendant was offered a plea agreement that allowed him to serve only eighteen months with five years probation. The man had actually only served five months and was released when the prison system reached its maximum capacity during the Christmas holidays. The jailers were required to either release inmates or pay a fine.

Just as Jennifer's hand released the "On" button for the coffee pot, the kitchen phone rang.

"Hello," she grumbled. Who would be calling at this hour? It was to early for the phone to be ringing. She needed coffee and she needed to think about what all of this meant.

"Jen, did you see the paper?" asked Jamie. "Isn't it great, they got him? He's in jail. My God, I feel so much better."

"Yes, I saw the article but remember, Jamie, arrested is not convicted. We still have a long way to go," Jennifer reminded her friend. "Did you read the whole article? Jamie, I'm worried. What if this goes on forever? What if our boys have to get up in front of a room full of people and tell in detail what happened? Oh, what have we started?"

"Who cares? The rest will be easy. Jen, they believed us: the police, the court system, the grand jury. They must or they wouldn't have indicted him and arrested him," she crowed. "At least he can't get to our kids anymore. Thank God for that."

"But what if he only gets five months in jail; how fair is that?" Jennifer's call waiting buzzed. "Jamie, I've got another call on the other line. I'll call you back later today. Just keep your fingers crossed that everything goes well. Bye." She hung up "Hello?" she said again, immediately.

"Did you see the article in the paper, isn't it great? They arrested Larry Cunningham." It was Joyce and she sounded like she had won the lottery.

"Yes, I saw it. I was just on the phone with Jamie. I was surprised that it happened so fast," Jennifer said. With the phone tucked between her shoulder and ear, she was able to get the coffee made and drank a cup and then another before she actually got off the phone.

For the next four hours, Jennifer was on the phone with every one of the other mothers. The worst call of the day was from her ex-husband, Jacob's father, who had somehow gotten a copy of the Mobile paper and couldn't wait to add his two cents. Jennifer had called her ex-husband the night they first reported it to Wes and they had several conversations after that. This conversation was much the same as their last five conversations about what had happened. He was angry, wanting to kill this "pervert," wondering how in the world Jennifer could have let this happen. Didn't she spend time with their son, didn't she keep an eye on him and who he was hanging out with? Jacob's father had made it seem that it was all Jennifer's fault that this had happened. It seemed that somehow she should have known and should have done something to stop it. She knew in her head that it was crazy to think that, but her heart told her that she should have done something, should have known some how.

Around eleven, Jennifer called Wes to say thank you. She let him know that all the mothers appreciated his handling of the investigation.

"Thanks for everything. I think that you talking to the boys made all the difference. They really look up to you and your position" said Jennifer.

"You're very welcome, Jennifer. I'm just glad that I was there for the boys. You know it takes a great deal of courage for kids that age to recognize and report situations like this," Wes assured her. "And it's not over yet. There's still a long way to go. Arresting people is sometimes the easy part. The kids still have to get through the trial. I'm sure the DA's office will be in contact with you when they need statements and need to prep the kids."

"I know, I read the article. It's actually kind of scary that this creep could only get a couple of months for what he did to the kids," she said.

"Don't think about that part at this point. Just keep the kids safe and away from the press. Let them be kids for a while; this whole load of crap will definitely take the fun out of their lives when it all gets started," added Wes, knowing that he wasn't really helping the situation but wanting to warn Jennifer about what was to come.

As Wes was talking to Jennifer on the phone, he looked up as a shadow fell over his desk. It took a minute but Wes put the name and the face together. Before him stood Tim Cunningham, Larry's brother.

"Hello, Wes. How are you?" Tim said. Tim put out his hand as Wes hung up the phone. Wes had heard a lot about Tim and he had to admit that it was all good. Tim ran a good church, except for the current situation. Wes understood that a family could be a good one but have a black sheep that got it in trouble. You really couldn't hold the brother responsible for what Larry Cunningham had done.

"Tim, what can I do for you? I'm a little surprised to see you in here. You know that I can't tell you anything or talk to you about your brother's case."

"I need to see my brother. I understand that he's in the jail. I'd like to speak with him as soon as convenient." Tim looked tired, like a hundred-pound weight was on his shoulders. Tim had always been a straight-up, confident guy who knew that he was on the side of goodness and joy. Today, he looked sad, beaten down. He may have been a man of God but this burden was too much even for him.

"I don't want any favors, Wes. I just need to see him. He's always been my responsibility, you know. I just can't believe that any of this is true. We're getting an attorney to try to sort it all out. You know kids have great imaginations. The best my wife and I can figure, the kids must have gotten upset about something that happened at camp and well, you know how kids are. TV and all, they learn some pretty crazy stuff, even in the movies. We just don't understand how this could happen."

"Let me see what I can do, Tim. Have a seat over by that wall and I'll be right with you," Wes said.

Tim moved to the guest chairs like a man much older than his years. As he sat down he put his hand on the bottom of the chair and lowered himself into the chair, very cautiously, holding onto the metal arms on the chair like an old man. Tim, not yet fifty years old, moved like a man of seventy.

Wes picked up the phone and dialed the jail next door. They assured him that Larry Cunningham had been processed and was currently in a temporary holding cell but he would be placed in his room shortly. They advised that any visitors be asked to wait another couple of hours until they could get the processing completed and made sure that the new celebrity inmate was completely at home in his new surroundings.

The jail guard let Wes know that the press was already asking questions about Larry and his situation. "What had he said?" "Had he confessed anything?" The normal stuff that the press liked to use to grab headlines. Wes was assured that no one was speaking to the press. He thanked the guard and let Tim know that his brother was being processed. If he could just want for a little longer, he would get him over to the jail to see his brother.

CHAPTER 13

▼

Larry sat down at the steel-topped table and looked across the room at the door. The interview room at the County jail was only slightly larger than his cell. The Baldwin County jail was remodeled in 1998 and had had two additions since then. The growth in the jail populations was a direct effect of the population growth for all of Baldwin County. After Hurricane Frederick in 1979, developers and landowners on the coast of Alabama, Mississippi, and the Florida Panhandle discovered that there was money in "that there sand." So the building explosion of the 1980s began. During the 1980s and 1990s, every square inch of sandy sugar white beach in Gulf Shores and Orange Beach, Alabama had been sold, subdivided, and resold several times over. Condominiums were built, and what used to be sleepy little fishing villages became an active little drinking villages in the 1980s. With the condos came the tourists, and with the tourists, came the bars. With the bars came all sorts of stupid criminal activities that the Redneck Riviera had held to a minimum in the past.

The jail systems in the small towns were reinforced, but the majority of the true criminal populations still had to be transported to Bay Minette for holding until the busy court system could catch up with the increased traffic. In addition to the general growth in the drinking population in the south part of the county, the drug cookers and distributors had also seen an increase in business with the tourist trade. So the jails were crowded. They continued to be overcrowded to the point that the authorities were forced to review the overall condition of the jails. The State of Alabama prison system began to transfer prisoners to jails in Mississippi and Georgia in 2003. The overpopulation caused unsanitary conditions at the prisons, and the State of Alabama made sure that its inmates were comfortable; including cable TV. A great many Alabamians couldn't afford cable TV with movie channels but criminals got their cable.

The State of Alabama had to pay the other states and local government facilities for the Alabama prisoners when they used County or other state facilities to house their prisoners. This lack of facilities continued to be a political platform for any judge or politician that could get the cameras pointed toward them. Everybody knew that it was a problem, but nobody had any great plans how to fix it.

So, when Larry arrived at the county jail from the city jail, the conditions were already past capacity. A facility that should have held only five hundred fifty prisoners held six hundred and thirty. Life became unbearable for the guards and the inmates at around six hundred. In rooms that generally held six to eight prisoners, portable bunk beds had been moved in to accommodate another four prisoners in each room. The increase in prisoners, however, did not result in an increase in the number of guards. Not even the new camera tracking system kept everybody safe. There were just too many people in too small a space.

Under normal circumstances, Larry would have been placed in a cell by himself. The everyday criminal hated child molesters more than any other criminal. It was well known that there was a hierarchy of criminals, and that child molesters were the lowest form of life in the population. This placed Larry in a potentially dangerous situation. With the added news coverage and the celebrity that went with it, the general prisoners weren't impressed with Larry Cunningham. Many of the prisoners had found God during their time in prison, and Larry's claim to be a man of God and an indicted child molester, that was not a good combination.

The jail population was separated by types of crime, which meant that the worst of humanity was housed with the worst of humanity. Larry had spent the past fourteen hours with three other inmates in a ten by six cell with four beds and an open toilet area. The doors to the cells are all open with bars only. The surveillance system was set up so that each cell could be monitored in a continuous loop. The inmates would have to know the timing of the camera system to get away with anything without being seen. There was no place in the cell to have any privacy. This was for the guards as well as the inmates. If the guards couldn't see, inmates get hurt. If an inmate spent enough time at the facility they could find ways to get a little privacy, but these spaces were minimal and that was good for the inmates like Larry Cunningham, child molester.

Inmates in Baldwin County were dressed by color code. The guards knew quickly who to watch out for if anything happened. Inmates who may have been a threat to themselves were dressed in orange cotton jumpers that snapped up the front. The orange jumper guys looked the part of the loser criminal.

Violent criminals were dressed in red jumpers. If the shit hit the fan in the jail, the guards were given permission to Taser the red jumpers first and ask questions later. The red jumper guys looked nothing but scary.

Nonviolent criminals were dressed in blue jumpers; they look like they were in regular uniforms and were maybe maintenance men or jailors. And any inmates who had been in the jail system for awhile, been well behaved, were not violent, and have earned special status by behaving themselves and stayed out of trouble, were dressed in white cotton shirts and white cotton pants. They looked like painters. This group worked for the jail in maintenance or doing laundry and janitorial services. They were allowed to leave the jail on work programs and even allowed to do shopping at the Dollar Store on rare occasions. It was an earned privilege and not easily achieved. These inmates were paid for their work and could use this stipend to pay off the debts they may have accrued due to their crimes.

Larry wore an orange jumper, not because anyone believed that he would do anything to himself, but knowing his crime, the jailers believed that he needed the extra visibility. His had been a very public arrest, on all the news channels, and within the first hours, Larry had been approached by several guards who needed to let him know what a dead man he was, and how pleasant they planned to make his visit. Larry had also been the target of several inmates who felt the need to communicate with Larry very vocally as he entered the jail block. Guards were big gossips and they'd prepared everyone for this fallen man of God who liked to play touchy feely with seven-year-old boys. There was no lower form of life than that.

Larry looked up as the door to the interview room opened and in walked Larry's brother, Tim. The pastor looked around the small interview room with an expression on his face like he smelled something that he didn't much care for. The walls were covered with a washed-out yellow paint that the county had gotten for a very good price several years before. The color had faded to that of pale urine, and the jail's smell matched the color.

Tim studied the room before he looked at his brother. His gaze fell on Larry in a questioning manner, his expression one of wonder. He wasn't sure this man before him was the same guy that he had grown up with and had known all his life. Tim studied Larry for several moments without a word.

Larry broke the silence. "Tim, thank God," Larry said, moving to hug his brother.

"Sit still, Larry" the deputy who had come in with the visitor said. "You're not allowed any physical contact with any guest. Sit back down, please." The deputy was extremely cordial compared to how others had acted. Larry understood this cordial approach was out of respect for his guest and not for him.

"No problem," said Larry.

Larry sat back down at the steel table and looked across at his brother. Tim took the seat across the table.

Tim was the older than Larry by twenty-four months. When they were growing up, it was always Larry who got all the attention. Larry was the better looking of the two. Unlike Larry, Tim was tall but overly thin, and when he put on his church robes, he looked a lot like the ghost of Christmas Past, only year-round. Tim was not an attractive thin either, but a "you need to eat Big Macs every day for the next year" thin. Tim's hair was red. Larry had red highlights during the summer when he spent so much time in his garden. Larry had a perfect, even tan; Tim looked red and burnt during the summer. The two had the same facial features but where Larry made them look attractive, Tim made them look comfortable.

When it came to grades, Larry was the little brother who never studied. Tim was the older brother whose grades were a little bit higher but through exponential effort. Tim had always been jealous of Larry in an unnatural way. Everything always seemed so easy for Larry, and Tim had to work for everything he got. Larry was the extrovert, Tim shy and introverted. The only place that Tim was extroverted was in his church. Larry was a natural athlete, Tim was a bookworm.

Tim had a couple of things on Larry, though. Tim was happily married to his high school sweetheart. A lovely girl, pretty, and with a quick wit, a natural smile and a kindness inherent in preachers' wives. Tim was a good husband, a great father to his own kids who were now grown and he was a highly respected minister. He felt his religion to his core. He could feel God's grace in the cells of his body. There was nothing fake or pretend about him or his small family. When he got to the pearly gates, he was going to arrive via the express pass in the fast lane. No questions asked. Tim was forgiving, not at all a political preacher like most in his region. Tim Cunningham was good to his core and everyone who came in contact with him felt his grace instantly and deeply.

Tim sat and looked at his brother across the metal table. Larry's hands were casual at his side and he seemed relaxed. Tim had been to the jail many times professionally, but this time felt very different. This was his only brother. His only brother, who was accused of sexually molesting children from his flock, children who were under Tim's care and guidance.

"Larry, what happened? Please tell me what they're saying is as crazy as it sounds," Tim started off. His eyes had dark circles under them; he looked like he had aged ten years in the last forty-eight hours.

"How are the kids, Tim?" asked Larry, with genuine concern. "Have you talked to any of the boys? Jacob? Chris? Mikey?"

Tim looked at his brother, temporarily confused by the unexpected question. He paused because the question caught him off guard; he was trying to figure out why Larry was asking and, more importantly, why he didn't immediately deny the charges against him.

"No, Larry, I haven't seen the boys yet. I did get a visit from Jamie. She was saying that when you took all the boys to camp, they came up with this crazy story about you sexually abusing them. All of them. Well, not all, but most of them, seven of them." Tim dropped all of this on the table like a bomb from a B-52. There, he felt better, now that he had said it and gotten it out in the open.

"But are the kids okay? None of them have been taken anywhere? None of them have run away, have they?" pleaded Larry.

Tim stared at this man he should have known so well. He moved slowly in the chair, trying to get more comfortable. He sat up straight and folded his hands in front of him. He thought that he had to get control of himself, and put on his preacher face. Tim took a deep breath and tried to look at the man across the table as just another member of his church family.

"No. Listen, you're my brother and I plan to get you out of here. I'll get an attorney; we've already talked to Bayless Barlett. I'll pay for him myself if I need to. Your church family will stand by you. Believe me, everyone knows what great imaginations these kids have." Tim laughed, but only for effect; there was no joy or humor behind the laugh. "These kids, Shawn, Jacob, Darren. They've all been in trouble before, and they can't make up lies about one of our church family like this." Tim wanted to reach across the table to touch his brother's hand for comfort but remembered the guard watching from the door.

Tim got no response: not a thank you or good idea or a kiss my ass. His baby brother sat across the table, head down, shoulders slumped, a rejected shell of a man studying the floor, or perhaps his feet in white shower slippers that the County issued. Larry mumbled something so low that Tim couldn't even make it out.

"What?" Tim whispered back to his brother. "What did you say, Larry? I didn't hear you."

A rap at the door to the interview room made Tim look up. The guard, who had been standing just outside the door, popped into view through the window and he peered in at them, looking cautiously at what they were doing.

"Two minutes, guys ... Two minutes," said the guard, moving away from the door but not too far away in case something happened.

"Please give us a few minutes," Tim said to the guard, turning back to Larry who still studied his slippers. "What did you say?" Tim again whispered, "What did you just say?" He leaned over the table as much as he thought the guard would allow, getting closer to Larry to hear what he had to say. "You need to talk to me Larry; I need to know what really happened. Do you have any idea why these boys would be making all these lies up about you?"

Larry mumbled something again as he put his face in his hands and began to cry. "Those kids love me. I did everything for those kids." Larry's tears fell through his hands and onto the dirty table. "I was the closest thing most of them had ever had to a father. I would have done anything for them. I protected them, loved them, cared for them."

Tim took the chance and put his hand on Larry's bent shoulders. "I know Larry, that's why I can't understand why they would do this to you. Lie about you this way."

The tears really started to fall, and Larry sobbed into his hands. Tim would have loved to move around the table and put his arm around his brother, but he didn't want to break the rules and be thrown out. They both sat quietly, at a loss for what to say or do. Larry continued to cry softly, and Tim wondered why he wasn't mad about this injustice. Why was he not talking to Tim about getting him out of this place? This damn defeatist attitude was an unproductive waste of time and so unlike his little brother. Larry was a fighter for the truth, why wasn't he fighting now? Tim started to ask the questions when he heard the guard put the key in the door lock.

"Okay guys, time's up," said the guard, opening the door. The keys in the lock clanked and the door squeaked as the guard entered the room. Tim needed more time. He needed another ten minutes to get Larry talking. He felt there was so much to say and wondered why his brother was not talking to him. Didn't he understand the mess he was in?

Tim stood to leave, bent down at the knees, knelt in front of Larry, and said a quick prayer. The guard moved closer but allowed Tim to get away with it. They'd been briefed that Tim was a minister, and the guard thought it was probably okay. Not a religious man himself, he felt a little uncomfortable, so he lowered his head out of respect for the minister, not the inmate. The guard waited while Tim finished his prayer and got to his feet.

"Amen." Tim stood and patted his brother's shoulder one more time. As he turned to leave, Larry mumbled something. This time Tim was close enough to Larry to understand what his beloved brother said.

"Tim, believe the kids," said Larry, looking up at Tim with tears in his eyes.

Tim stopped and looked Larry squarely in his eyes for the first time since he entered the room.

"Save it for another day, dude," said the guard, reaching for Tim's arm and pulling him gently toward the door. The guard stepped between the two men to break up the conversation and directed the minister to the door.

Tim pushed back into the interview room past the guard. "What did you say, Larry? What did you just say?"

"Let's go, Red. I don't care if you are a priest or something," said the guard. He reached out for Tim's arm to lead him from the room.

"Larry, what did you just say?" Tim tugged away from the guard to get closer to his brother.

"Believe the kids, Tim. Believe the kids," said Larry, just loud enough to be heard.

Tim hesitated and looked at this man that he thought he knew well, as if seeing him for the very first time. He was frozen, with a hundred questions on his lips but no chance of asking any of them now.

The guard picked this time to show he meant business, giving Tim a good tug to get him out of the interview room. Tim, who was suddenly too dizzy to even speak, followed the guard down the hall. He found himself in the lobby before his head cleared, and he could think. When the door was locked behind him, he realized that he was standing alone in a drab pea green reception area. He moved slowly, as if still in a trance, not able to get the words out of his head. "Believe the kids." Did he really say, "Believe in the kids?" As in, protect the kids for me? Take care of the kids? Did he mean "believe in the kids?"

No, Tim didn't think that was what Larry meant at all. "Believe the kids." Was that the answer to his question about why would the kids would lie about what the police were saying? Surely he had misunderstood, or perhaps Larry had misunderstood what Tim was trying to get him to explain. That was it. This was all a huge misunderstanding. But no matter how hard Tim tried to justify what his brother had understood or which question he answered, he was very afraid that he had just heard his brother confess to molesting seven of the children who had been placed in his care by the Lutheran Church.

As Tim walked through the door of the county jail and into the parking lot, the bright sun light blinded his eyes for an instant but cleared his mind. He knew exactly what Larry meant. "Believe the kids."

Wes Harmon sat on the hood of his car. "Hey, Tim. How'd it go? You get a confession for me? Make my job a lot easier." Wes laughed at his attempt to lighten the moment. Wes could tell that the minister had been shaken by whatever he saw or heard in the jail.

It took Tim a minute to register who Wes was. Tim thought that this must be what Alice in Wonderland felt like when she fell through that rabbit hole. Everything was confusing and surreal. Tim's mind raced back to the conversation with Larry, thinking about the article that had been in the newspaper, thinking about his conversation with Jamie that morning, and wondering just where the truth began, and the fantasy ended. Trying to remember what questions he had asked Larry. What was he answering with that last comment? Could he have heard what Larry was saying correctly, and what did it mean?

"Tim, you don't look so good. Everything go okay with Larry?" Wes moved up to Tim and placed a hand on his shoulder. Wes waited, giving Tim a moment he obviously needed to collect himself. He wondered what could have caused this confusion and finally asked the question. He needed to know more for his own case than out of concern for either of these guys. "Tim, did Larry say anything to you about this mess? Anything at all that might help us find out what's really going on here?"

Tim just stared at Wes as if he didn't really understand who he was or what he was doing here at all. "No," said Tim. He was thinking now, his mind racing. This was the police; he needed to get it together before he did something crazy. "Nothing that makes any sense, I mean difference. Nothing that makes any difference. Larry is a good man, Wes. My brother is a good man. He's in a situation right now that no man should ever have to face. He has always been a man of God; he cares deeply for all the children in the church. Our parents raised us both to do God's work. My brother is not a monster, not anything like the press or the media are saying. The truth will prevail and we know that God will sort it out in the end."

Tim turned away from Wes and started across the parking lot to his own car. "Yes, they made sure that we all knew our responsibilities to do God's work." Tim muttered under his breath, barely loud enough for Wes to hear.

CHAPTER 14

▼

In a normal criminal investigation, the police got the information about a crime from several sources and they investigated the crime. When they had enough to convince a member of the district attorney's staff that they can prove the case, the DA took the evidence to the grand jury. If the grand jury indicted, the police picked the criminal up and threw his behind in the Baldwin County jail.

Within a very short period of time, the indicted criminal must appear before the court for a sentencing date. Larry Cunningham had only been in jail a short time, and he would be appearing in court today.

Katie had worked last weekend doing an orientation, so she had a day off in the middle of the week. Today was Wednesday, which was a slow day in her world, and a great day to take off and get her errands done. Working weekends sucked but if she got to the grocery, bank, driver's license office, and places like that during the week without any crowds, working the weekend had its perks. Katie noticed on yesterday's news broadcast that Larry would be appearing in court today. Morbid curiosity brought her to the courtroom to watch the action firsthand rather than waiting for the nightly new to tell her what had happened. Katie didn't have a real reason to be there; she was just curious.

It was only 9:00 a.m. and Katie was working on her second cup of Joe Muggs coffee when she walked into the courtroom. It seemed that a lot of people had the same morbid curiosity that she did about this case. The courtroom was packed when she walked in and she looked around for a place to sit. She had no idea when Larry Cunningham's case would be called and sitting down sounded like a good idea.

She couldn't find a place so she moved up the aisle to the front of the room. There were cops and people who look like lawyers everywhere. She saw an empty seat in the third row. She started to climb over the seven people already sitting. "Why did people refuse to move to the middle, making her climb over them?" she wondered. She tried to be careful since she had hot coffee in her hand. She made it to an empty seat, next to a good-looking guy in a sheriff's uniform and when she turned to sit down, her purse caught on the seat in front of her, yanking her arm and the coffee cup backwards. She didn't drop the cup, managed to hang onto the purse, and didn't fall into the lap of the sheriff. She did splash Baldwin County's finest with Joe Muggs's finest. She saw an upturned face with wonderful eyes. She smiled and started to apologize. He smiled back and took a handkerchief out of his pocket.

"Good thing I like Joe Muggs," said the cop as he wiped the coffee off his uniform.

It wasn't a lot of coffee, but Katie noted that he would need to go home and change clothes or everybody would think that he was a slob. "Sorry," Katie said about a thousand more times as she took her seat.

Wes Harmon noticed that the coffee lady wasn't bad to look at, as she took the seat next to him. She wore old, faded jeans that fit snuggly with a white sweater and Keds sneakers. Not a bad look though the Keds sneakers were a bit unusual for a woman her age. When she finally sat down and got comfortable, he noticed that she smelled good, too. Wes leaned a little to his left to get a better smell at the same time that she turned to look at him. Their faces were only inches apart. The expression on both of their faces seemed to say that the distance wasn't making them nervous, but the energy between them was. Now it was Wes's turn to apologize to Katie.

"Sorry, I just love the smell of coffee," he mumbled trying to cover the fact that it was her hair and not the coffee that smelled so good.

"Sure you do," Katie said. She gave him a smile that said, "I ain't buying it, mister."

The bailiff called the courtroom to order. "All rise!" Katie and Wes stood with the hundred other people in the courtroom, for the arrival of Judge Black. Katie recognized the DA as he hurried into the courtroom just behind the judge, and it appeared that his entire staff was with him.

Wes knew immediately that something wasn't right. Everybody looked like they have been in the back chambers eating green frogs. Judges always looked slightly sour; when a Judge was sworn in they promised to always look sour and serious when wearing the black robe. Now Judge Black looked downright pissed.

Wes didn't know what was going on. Black didn't just stroll into the courtroom as he usually did. Today, Judge Black stomped up the three steps to his bench like someone about to defend his own personal character.

The DA, a man who should have been in his element at this moment, with the news cameras and press at the back of the courtroom, appeared to have been the source of whatever had pissed off the judge. The assistant DA, Matt, Katie remembered from the grand jury. He looked like he might cry. Judy Hooks had on her best poker face; Wes couldn't tell a thing from her expression. Wes had watched these four people for several years and knew that something was about to happen. With what he was seeing, it wasn't going to be good.

"Ladies and gentlemen, please be seated," Judge Black said, just a little too loud. The clerk sitting next to him looked up and actually jumped in her seat. "Sorry, Ms. Cindy, didn't mean to scare you" The judge nodded to the bailiff who called, "Larry Cunningham."

Wes thought the bailiff must have eaten one of the green frogs too. He appeared extremely bitter as he spit out the name. Wes had known that bailiff for years and had never seen him show emotion in the courtroom. When someone had been a bailiff for as long as that guy, nothing fazed them that happened in the court. Something was very wrong if this bailiff was unhappy.

Larry Cunningham was escorted into the room by two police officers from a back door. As Larry came in, the mumbling of the crowd in the courtroom got louder and louder. It seemed that more people than just Larry sensed that something was amiss, and the chatter had already started in the room. He was placed at the table in the front with the man who must have been his attorney. Larry wore a tailored black suit with a white shirt and a conservative red and yellow tie.

This was the first time that Katie had seen Larry Cunningham, and she was surprised that he was so handsome. Then she remembered that several mass murderers had been described as good-looking, which helped them get their victims to go along. Good-looking people had an advantage, even when they were evil.

Judge Black sat in his chair and stared at Larry Cunningham with nothing less than pure contempt. Then the judge leaned back in his chair and studied his hands. Judge Black was not a man to twiddle away time in the courtroom. He had a caseload that demanded he kept things moving all day, every day. He sat for a moment longer, staring at the defendant across the room from him. Larry squirmed in his seat like a kid in the principal's office. His attorney looked down, not understanding what was going on, and thought that the papers in front of him were safer to look at than this pissed off judge. So Larry's attorney became totally interested in the blank sheets on his writing pad. The people at the DA's table weren't moving a muscle. They didn't even appear to be real; they looked more like wax dummies than seasoned professional attorneys.

"I can't believe I'm doing this," Judge Black said. He sat forward in his chair and picked up a pen. He studied the pen as if it was the first one that he'd ever seen, turning it over and over in his fingers, clicking the cartridge several times. "I've spent a lot of years on this bench, Mr. Cunningham. A lot of years. I've seen things and heard testimony, stories really, about things that no decent, educated man should ever have to hear or see. And I must say that 99 percent of the time, justice is served by this court and the system works. Sometimes justice is served cold, when we can't get the criminal to court for several years. Sometimes it's served hot, because the matters brought to me are so emotional that I can barely keep the community from lynching the criminal, even in this day and age. But the justice system in this state and this country generally works." The judge sat back hard in his chair; again, he studied the pen in his hand.

Judge Black was not a tall man, and when he sat all the way back in his chair on his elevated platform, he could barely be seen. From the public's seating, if you were in the front several rows, you might only see the top of his head. He sat this way for full three minutes, still studying this mystical thing called an ink pen. Three minutes didn't seem like a long time unless you sat in the courtroom, waiting for information. The people in the audience started to fidget. Law enforcement officers instinctively put their hands on their guns as they stood around the edges of the courtroom. Members of the public reached over to loved ones to hold their hands. The judge appeared to be thinking of anything he could do in order to not have to say the words he was thinking.

Katie looked over at Matt, sitting at the DA's table. He looked at his hands and his head was so low, it almost touched the table. Judy sat straight as a board next to Matt, stone still, staring at the judge without blinking. Her face showed none of the emotion that was so obvious in Matt's face.

DA Whitman turned in his chair and sat sideways with his feet out in the middle of the aisle, his back to Matt and Judy. His elbows were on his knees and his hands were clasped as if in prayer. He looked at the floor in front of him. Whitman was generally confident and commanding in the courtroom, but now he looked like he has just been told that a ton of cement blocks had been dropped on his Mercedes, and he had forgotten to pay the insurance.

Something was very wrong.

Finally, the judge sat up again but didn't look at Larry Cunningham. "Mr. Cunningham, the charges that brought you to this courtroom today have been dropped. You are free to go." Judge Black banged his gavel on the desk and sat back even lower in his chair.

There was complete and total silence in the courtroom as if everyone in the courtroom froze. Mouths hung open; nobody moved, nobody breathed.

Finally, a woman seated at the back of the room, stood up and screamed. "WHAT?" That did it; the logjam was broken and pandemonium broke out in the courtroom. A row of women stood up next to the one who screamed at the judge. "What did you say? What did he say, Jennifer?" She asked the women sitting next to her. "Did you hear what he said? I didn't hear what he said." The first woman screamed over and over.

"Calm down, Jamie" said a women sitting next to her.

"This is bullshit" yelled another one of the women sitting in the group.

The law enforcement officers, who had been leaning against the wall, stood up straight and looked around in confusion.

Katie recognized the women in the back were the mothers who were brave enough to bring Larry Cunningham to this place for judgment. There was crying and talking all around the courtroom. Some of the attendees with press badges moved to the back of the courtroom, running for the door.

Everyone was yelling. People moved out of their seats and into the aisle. Several people, who looked like grandparents, uncles, and fathers, walked to the front of the courtroom and began screaming at the judge. The law enforcement presence was big, and they are all on their feet, moving to the front, to help the judge and his staff. The bailiffs got Larry Cunningham and his lawyer hustled out the back door. The judge sat back in his chair and lowered his head in his hands. The DA and his assistants were all frozen, as if in shock.

After what seems like forever but in truth was only a minute, Judge Black banged his gavel and walked out of the room. Nobody heard what he growled, but if you were a lip reader, you would have learned a new phrase that would have embarrassed his proud mother.

CHAPTER 15

▼

The chaos from Judge Black's announcement that Larry Cunningham was a free man started out slowly. Larry had been out of the news for a few days, so it would take the general media a minute to dust off the Cunningham file and pull up the old video from his arrest. The monster had used his fifteen minutes of fame, and they had filed him away as old news, just another sexual predator that was going to jail. But a sexual predator that was loose on the streets? That was news.

The reaction in the courtroom was quick. Sitting in the court room that day, was the member of the press who had also been on the grand jury, Lindsey Loiselle. Lindsey was a Bay Minette girl, and was discontented to have this important job in her hometown, she thought she should have been bigger and more important. Lindsey had recently married Norborne Stowe, her high school sweetheart. Her refusal to change her name was a show of her independence. She felt that, as a professional writer, she had already started to make a name for herself, and after two years with the paper, she decided to stay with Loiselle. Readers knew her name on the byline and she felt that changing her name would be losing ground.

Lindsey had sat next to Katie Race for two weeks, where she and the other members had heard in detail the horrible things that Larry Cunningham had done to the "Lutheran Kids." She had done the right thing and done a good job of staying out of the whole "Arrest of a Monster." She knew that it was her responsibility to protect the confidentiality of what she knew.

Lindsey had done a great deal of additional research on Larry Cunningham after her grand jury experience, and her first article about him had hit the paper this morning. She had been able to work in facts she learned on the grand jury, but she was sure that everyone would write them off as being her good research. She had used the information she heard in the grand jury about material and notes that had been found by the sheriff's deputies the night that Larry was arrested in her article. She had no way of knowing that this information was protected because it had not been correctly documented at the time and therefore would never been submitted to the court. She had also disclosed information about the discussion that the children had at camp, this was also protected information due to their ages and was not admissible in court. The information that she had published in her article was only for the grand jury but Larry's attorney had been able to get the judge to throw out the case due to this leak of information by Lindsey. The article had been published that morning and everything seemed fine, until this happened anyway.

Lindsey was taking notes when the judge had entered the room. Her expression was reserved and professional but her eyes showed concern. Lindsey had watched many court proceedings over the last several months, and recognized that something was very wrong with the DA and the judge. An otherwise boring morning in court had gotten very interesting. The announcement that Cunningham was being released caused Lindsey to break the number one rule of the Baldwin County Court System: no cell phones in the courtroom. Lindsey immediately grabbed her phone, dialed the number for her office, and asked to speak to the editor.

"In a meeting?" she yelled at the secretary on the other end. "I don't give a shit if he is in a meeting. Get his ass on this phone now!" Lindsey stood up as chaos broke out in the courtroom.

"Oh my God, what have I done?" said Lindsey as she quickly looked around the courtroom. Several ladies in the back were screaming and crying. Judge Black stormed out of the courtroom like a tornado. She had never seen a judge storm out of his own courtroom before. DA Whitman sat at the table with his head in his hands. The assistant DA stood and loaded paperwork into a brown file folder and put several black binders into a briefcase, obviously pissed off.

Lindsey knew she had a big story. Hell, she probably was the big story if anybody ever figured out what she had done. She looked around frantically, trying to take in everything at once. The screaming in the back of the courtroom was from a woman who looked vaguely familiar. It all clicked together.

The group of women was the mothers of the boys Larry Cunningham had abused. One of them, a dark-haired hippie-looking lady in her early forties, pushed her way through the crowd in the main aisle toward the front of the courtroom.

With her cell phone in one hand, Lindsey dug for her mini recorder with the other. The screaming woman had made her way to the front of the courtroom. She pushed through the swinging gate that separated the general public from the attorneys and defendant area. Bailiffs scrambled to get the mayhem under control and didn't notice that she grabbed Whitman by the front of his shirt.

"What happened, you son of a bitch?" Jamie screamed. "How could you? How did you screw this up?"

David Whitman stood there, hands by his side, head slightly lowered, and a poker face that showed no sign of what he felt. As the bailiff reached for Jamie, she pushed David, shoving him backwards into the defense table.

As the bailiff turned Jamie away from the district attorney, Jennifer and Kim and the others reached her. "She's okay, let her go," Kim said to the bailiff. He still had both of Jamie's arms in a bear hug, "It's okay. She's all right now. You can let her go," Jennifer said, reaching for his hands and trying to loosen his grip on Jamie.

As the bailiff let go of Jamie, she crumbled into Jennifer's arms and began to cry. All the ladies sat down in the front row of the seats to keep from falling over on themselves.

Whitman leaned on the table for a minute longer. Matt reached out for him, putting his hand on his shoulder. "Come on, Boss, we're done here." The bailiff moved over to the district attorney to make sure that he was okay and gently pushed him toward the back door that he entered less than twenty minutes ago.

Lindsey pushed through the crowd to get to somebody, anybody. She needed to find out what happened here. What was the story? Did this have anything to do with the article that she had published that morning? She needed to get to the district attorney. Other members of the press pushed and shoved their way to the front of the courtroom. Everyone yelled questions at David, at Matt, at anybody who would listen.

The mothers were all surrounded by the press, and without understanding what she was saying, Jamie yelled, "I'll kill the bastard before I let him get away with it." The whole room went dead silent, and the cameras turned toward this woman who would later be identified as one of the mothers. This outburst would be replayed on the nightly news over hundreds of stations in the next several weeks.

Down the street at the Daily Grind coffee shop, the locals watched the midday news on the TV in the corner. As the words "breaking news" were posted in the upper right hand corner of the screen, the face of Larry Cunningham showed on the screen.

"Hey, you guys, shut up a minute!" hollered Harry Wilson over the chatter about the upcoming high school football season. Everyone turned to the TV to see what Harry was watching.

"Breaking news at this hour in the much-publicized child abuse case of Larry Cunningham. It appears from early reports, that all charges against Cunningham have been dropped. Cunningham was a youth minister at the Loxley Lutheran Church, and was indicted for sexually abusing seven boys under the age of eleven in his church," said the noonday reporter.

"What?" Jim Howe jumped to his feet from the bar stool he sat on at the cash register. He turned up the volume. "You have got to be kidding me!" He walked toward the TV before he even realized that the cash register stood open from the last transaction.

Larry's picture disappeared, and the report went live to the Baldwin County Courthouse. A News Ten reporter was with David Whitman. "Mr. Whitman, can you give us any idea why Mr. Cunningham has been released from custody at this hour, and why all the charges had been dropped against him?"

"Look, it was just one of those things." David, with a red face, visibly shaken by the last several minutes, was uncharacteristically out of control. He was a man who controlled his emotions better than a daytime soap opera star, but right now he looked like he could eat the heads off the reporters, whoever they are. "We worked as hard as we could to get this guy indicted. We had a solid case, and the Baldwin County Sheriff's Department did an excellent job of investigating and putting all the facts together. However, during the process of putting this together, a mistake was made. Information that was suppressed by the judge and that directly compromised Mr. Cunningham's right to a fair trial had been obtained by the media and made public."

"Mr. Whitman, I know that the community will be very concerned about Mr. Cunningham's freedom. Is there no way that you can continue with his trial? What happens to Mr. Cunningham now?" asked the reporter, knowing the answer before the question was even out of her mouth.

"Mr. Cunningham is a free man, as of this morning. He is free to do whatever he wishes, wherever he wishes. We have no other charges against this man, therefore, we can not hold him in this or any other jail," Whitman said. "Listen, I'm sick about this turn of events, too. Believe me, we would have loved to take Mr. Cunningham into a court of law and shone the light of justice on his actions. However, we have this form of government, which works 99 percent of the time to uphold justice; this was not one of those times. Occasionally, that one percent happens when the system works to protect the guilty from getting the justice they deserve." David moved slowly to the right, with the crowd of media right on his tail.

Whitman and the reporter continued to talk, but nobody listened to a word he said. All over the county, people relived what had happened and rehashed the facts. Larry Cunningham had sexually abused seven young kids in their community. The police had him dead to rights, no questions of guilt or innocence. He was a monster and he needed to go away.

By the time the six o'clock news was ready to go to production, the swarm of media flies had enough footage of toothless rednecks threatening to kill the guy in the name of justice to fill the whole news hour.

"You got to ask yourself, what's wrong with this world we live in when a pervert like this guy can walk out of jail and right back into his fancy house without anybody doing nothing about it?" asked Bubba Parsons from Robertsdale.

"Seems to me that somebody needs to do something about this and quick-like. These good ol' boys around these parts ain't about to let Mr. Cunningham fiddle with their sons no more. Not knowing what we know about this guy," said David Cotton from Silverhill.

"You know that the justice system must have had a very good reason to allow Mr. Cunningham his freedom. They know so much more than we do at this point. If the judge and district attorney didn't have enough evidence to hold Mr. Cunningham, well then, we need to accept that this is the reason for our system of government and move forward," added Emily Corte of Fairhope. The media always had to find one liberal to balance out the common sense of the general population.

The last shot on every newscast that night was the courtroom footage of Jamie being forcibly removed from the district attorney by the bailiff. Somewhere in the courtroom was a camera, probably from a cell phone with video that captured the whole ugly scene on tape. It had only taken a few minutes for Lindsey to recognize what was going on and hang up on her boss to switch over to the video feature on her phone. The footage was priceless. She even got close enough at the end to get Jamie screaming that she would "kill the bastard." It was assumed that by "the bastard" she meant Cunningham, when actually she meant Whitman.

*   *   *   *

Wes watched the drama in the courtroom firsthand. Police officers always worried that something like this would happen. The whole case was way too explosive. There were too many women and children involved, and the public was just shy of a public hanging before the judge entered the courtroom. Now that everything had come undone, Wes's immediate reaction was to find the closest drinking establishment opens at this hour.

Once the trouble started, it had been everything that Wes could do to elbow his way to the front of the courtroom to try to help the poor bailiffs and his fellow officers get the court officials out of the room ... Officers who weren't even on court duty helped push people toward the exits to get everyone out of the courtroom. Wes grabbed Cindy Plummer and got her safely out of the stampede. Half pulling, half carrying, he lifted Cindy around the waist, and using body blocking learned in his football days, had thrown himself and her through the back door of the courtroom and into the connecting hall.

Even the back hallway was crazy as everyone in the offices had rushed toward the courtroom to find out what all the noise was about. Judge Black stood fifteen feet down the hall, holding the Baldwin County sheriff by the shirt collar. "Get my courtroom back to order, *now*! Can't you bunch of fuck ups do anything right?"

As Wes put Cindy down, she fell more that walked into her office, crying. She slammed the door of the officer behind her and Wes heard her recounting the situation to the staff in the Clerk's office.

"Holy Crap! This place is a mess," Wes thought.

Wes spent the next hour sorting out the chaos and getting everyone out of the courthouse and back to their offices. Thank goodness nobody was hurt. Wes found all the Lutheran Kids' mothers still sitting in the courtroom, waiting for something else to happen. He got them out of the courthouse and into their cars, and convinced them all to go to Jennifer's house, promising that he would come by later to check on them.

CHAPTER 16

---▼---

To say that I, Katie Race the hard-charging business woman, thought of nothing else after that day would be a bit dramatic. I sat in that courtroom and heard the judge say that the charges had been dropped. I watched the pain and disbelief wash over those women as they fought mentally and physically to deal with the complete failure of the system they trusted. I felt that I personally had failed them. We didn't know what had happened but we knew that this wasn't over.

I went to work at the store and did my job, but I thought about Larry Cunningham and those boys a great deal. I cut my grass in the yard and planted my marigolds like I always did in the fall, and thought about Larry Cunningham and how we had been told he loved to work in his garden. I lay ceramic tile in my entryway of my house and remembered that we had been told as Grand Jurors about the loft that Larry had used as an indoor campsite to entertain the kids as part of his perverted seduction of them. I went to my parent's house for lunch on Sunday afternoons and thought about those kids trusting their youth minister. How he was their surrogate father in many ways and how he had taken advantage of those innocent minds. I kept up appearances as a totally normal person while slowly letting Larry Cunningham eat away at my soul.

Outwardly, you wouldn't have seen a change in anything about my life. Inwardly, however something shifted. It was almost physical, like when you had a bad back and you stand up too fast and you hear a click as the parts align again. That small shift, that little change in my soul, started me thinking that there was no one to call, no one left to report this horrible injustice. I was a doer and fixed people's situations for a living.

There was no other option. This monster had hurt these children and was walking the streets without any restrictions. He had taken away that innocent part of those kids that people only have when they're very young, and nobody was doing anything about it. He had done physical and mental damage that would never be fixed, and he needed to pay for that. And for these horrible actions, the grand jury had indicted him. We had done the right thing, followed the rules, and completed our part of the fair justice system. He had been taken into custody by our law enforcement. But due to a mistake on someone's part, which was the only thing the judge and district attorney's office would say, Larry Cunningham was a free man.

My dominos were falling before I realized they had been pushed. I had no other option; I couldn't stand by and do nothing. I needed to do something to make this right.

I thought about Cora and everything that had happened to her. Why had the people who had hurt her been allowed to go free? Yes, her father had gone to jail but for a charge that wasn't related to what he had done to his daughter. The man who had physically abused her had never paid for that crime. The scales of justice were totally unbalanced and I needed to do something about it.

I was not a killer of anything other than deer. I wasn't a crazy person; I was a stable person. I was a human resources manager and a foster parent, a trusted member of my community. I voted Republican for heaven's sake, and believed that doing things right was important. I paid my taxes and I didn't get speeding tickets. I may not have gotten to church every Sunday, but I believed in God and I believed in letting him sort things out generally but this time I helped.

I remember when I decided what I needed to do. It was early fall, and I was at the hunting camp for the club's work weekend. It was normal practice that every year the members of the Perdido River Hunting Club got together to prepare for the next season. We cleaned hunting houses, planted the food plots, and repaired any damages that happened over the spring and summer when nobody was around. With forty members and several spouses, it took two days to put everything in order for the next hunting season. We tried to do all the work during the late summer to have the food plots up and growing when deer season opened in late November. We always managed to turn this weekend into a fun time with massive amounts of beer and old stories dug up and retold. I sat on the tailgate of an F350 waiting for Alan Bryars to finish the last row of a food plot when Mark Crabtree rolled up in his pickup and shut off the engine.

"Hey, Kate, you guys about done here?" He walked over to the truck I was sitting on, holding a beer in one hand.

"Just about. Alan has about five more minutes and we'll be headed back to the camp." My job was easy this year. I followed the tractor around to the different food plots, and made sure that the fool driving the tractor didn't fall off and run over himself. I could already taste the hamburgers waiting at the camp and I needed one; it had been a long, hot day. I couldn't wait to get one in my hand. I'd been driving the truck behind the tractor for several hours and this meant that I had inhaled an acre of dirt since we hadn't seen rain in three weeks. A cold beer and a hamburger was just the ticket to end a beautiful day in the woods.

"You know, I was just thinking. I saw that Larry Cunningham guy the other day in your neck of the woods. Barbara Dee and I were up to the Farm Fresh Market in Robertsdale getting some steaks for dinner and there he was, big as day." Mark took off his hat and hit it against his knee to clean it off. Dust and dirt flew off the hat like my grandmother's powder puff. "It really seems that somebody should do something about that guy. He's has been out of jail for awhile now. I thought for sure he would've at least counted his self lucky and got the hell out of the area." Mark looked over at Alan on the tractor, who was almost finished with the food plot. "Hell, the guy sure would be easy to take out; he didn't even move from his house on Highway 55 where he has been living for years. Still goes to the same stores and does the same things. Of course, he did leave the church and the Fire Department fired him, but other than that, it seems that the guy just keeps on going. Doesn't seem fair somehow."

I saw Larry the next week at Burris, the local farmers market on the Wednesday following the work weekend at Perdido River. I don't know if it was the divine hand of God that caused our paths to cross or the Devil himself giving me an idea that would condemn my soul to hell. But there we were, standing in the checkout line. Larry was ahead of me with a basket full of produce. I stood three people back, with strawberries and salad fixins. I wasn't the only person who recognized Larry that day. It was very apparent several people recognized him and weren't cutting him any slack for what they believed to be true.

The cashier, a cute little girl of seventeen, asked, "Did you find everything you need?" before she even looked up. She froze, one of his apples in one hand and a small bag of grapes in the other. He pretended not to notice it but everyone else sure did. I imagined that he got this reaction a lot and had learned to deal with it. Recovering from the initial shock, she continued to ring up all his purchases. I couldn't hear the conversation, but Larry continued to talk and smile at the young cashier while she moved as quickly as possible to get him rung up and bagged. As he paid and moved out of the market area toward the parking lot, all eyes followed him across the gravel parking area to his beat-up blue Ford pickup.

I looked at the truck; his Alabama license's plate said, "Gods Kids."

"Pervert!" spat a woman to my right as he reached the truck and loaded his groceries in the back.

"Jerk's got a lot of nerve. 'Gods Kids.' Who the hell does he think he is? Does he think we're that stupid?" said a kid about nineteen years old who pushed a cart of watermelons to replenish the shelf out front. The customers all stopped and watched what was going on; the only customer seemingly unaware of the feelings of the crowd was Larry Cunningham himself.

"Gives me the creeps for sure," added the cashier who just finished ringing his purchases up. "He comes in here about once a week. I asked Mr. Burris if we could just refuse to wait on him, but he said that we had to wait on him just like everybody else." The cashier wiped her hands on a dish towel behind the counter. She is young and I wondered if she knew any of the families who were involved.

"I heard that he couldn't shop at Cain's Market or Winn Dixie anymore. Cain's manager threw him out and won't let him back in there. Mr. Cain said he had grandchildren and he didn't care what the judge said, he didn't care if the guy starved to death, he wasn't selling him nothing," said the watermelon stocker.

I paid quickly for my purchases and headed for my car. I threw everything in the back seat, not really thinking about what I was doing, and I followed him out of the parking lot. I had watched him get in his truck and pull out of the parking space.

It was just one more domino that had him turn south, which was the same way I went home. For some reason, I felt compelled to follow him. I had seen on TV that he lived out in the country in Silverhill, which was only one small town east of mine, but I didn't know exactly where his house was. When he turned right on Highway 55, so did I, but I stayed far enough back to not be as obvious as I felt.

"What am I doing?" I asked myself several times. "What am I, Nancy Drew now?" But I kept on driving, following the man I could not get out of my mind.

Larry crossed over Highway 104. I followed and we went about two miles south until he took a left on a shelled driveway which I thought must be his home. I could see the rooftop about one hundred yards off the road, but the trees blocked the house from view. I drove past the shelled drive and turned around on the next paved road. As I passed by the front of the house again, I noticed that his closest neighbor was more than a mile down the road.

Larry's yard was surrounded by pecan orchards on two of the four sides. The fourth side was Highway 55, a county two-lane highway. Not a very busy road even in the middle of the day. The term "highway" in the country was different than what city folks would think of as a highway. These were regular roads that were well traveled but not busy like a major interstate. These were country roads. School buses stopped at the end of these driveways to pick up kids in the morning, and the most traffic inconvenienced might be two or three cars on any given day.

Larry's house sat back so far that you couldn't see what was going on in the front yard. It was a brick home, apparently built in the early 1950s. The previous owners had built some additions to the main structure of the house, but it had changed little in fifty years. Back then, the primary source of water had been Polecat Creek and the bathroom had been the old outhouse in the yard. The bathroom had been upgraded to indoor plumbing in the 1960s.

At one time this house had been the home of a farm family named Lazzari from Silverhill. Mr. Lazzari had made good living growing pecans and at one point had owned the whole 1,000 area track. Over the years, Mr. Lazzari's kids had sold off the pecan orchard and the original homestead had eventually been sold to Larry Cunningham with only 10 areas of the original piece of land. It was a small house, only 1500 square feet but the best part of the house was a large country kitchen. The kitchen was old but big, you could picture the large Lazzari family with tons of stair step kids around the kitchen table at holidays. I could picture Mr. Lazzari walking into the kitchen at dusk and having all the kids sitting around the kitchen table doing homework, while Mrs. Lazzari worked on putting together a potato salad to go with the baked chicken I could almost smell in the oven.

A garage had been added to the main house some time after the initial construction. The garage was considerably newer that the brick part of the house and was made of vinyl siding. Larry had also added a storage building that wasn't connected to the house and it looked like it would contain lawn mowers and Weed Eaters. The porch on the front of the house was also a more recent addition to the home. The covered porch added curb appeal, and Larry had placed two rocking chairs on the front porch that gave it a homey look.

Baldwin County had grown from a farming community to a beach community in the 1970s. Gone were the pecan orchards and potato fields that made for a good day's pay and an honest living. Some of the cotton fields were still around but not many. The new money in this county was in sand. The beaches of Gulf Shores had drawn a lot of people into the community and I, for one, remembered when living on the eastern shore of Mobile Bay wasn't the cool place that it was today. Now it was everything we could do to keep the tourists from ruining our way of life and disrupting the peace and quiet. The schools were better than any-where else in south Alabama because of the beach revenue, and this made moving across the bay from Mobile a real plus for young families.

I remembered from the information that was presented to the grand jury that several of Larry's kids had been to his house, and that some of the sexual acts had taken place at this house or in the yard. The boys reported having sleepovers at Larry's house. I also understood why somebody with Larry's specific perversion would like this house, which was off the main road, and away from all the other houses. The trees were great cover for anything that happened: blocked from wondering eyes and ears. The kids reported a sleeping loft that looked out over the front yard.

Larry hadn't used the master bedroom when the kids stayed at his house. He had fashioned a camp in the loft and put up tents where the bed would have been. The kids always thought it was neat that they could look out the loft's six-foot triangle window on the front of the house. You could see anyone coming up the front driveway from the time they turned off the road. That beautiful win-dow seemed a little freaky now that I understood Larry used it as a lookout for anyone who may have seen what he was up to with his young victims.

I didn't understand, even at this point, what I was planning to do. My curios-ity about Larry hadn't been a conscious thought; I just thought that I had to know where he lived for some reason. However, my hunter's instinct made notes about his house and that it was far removed from both the road and the neigh-bors. I wondered if there was access from the rear of the house. I noted that I should find out if the back yard was as enclosed as the front yard and if it was as hidden and private as the front of the house.

CHAPTER 17

▼

It was Labor Day weekend. Larry Cunningham had been out of jail for several months and on my mind a lot more lately. It seemed that I kept running into him at the strangest times and places. This man, a complete stranger to me a year ago, seemed to turn up everywhere I went. I reminded myself that we both lived in a community with just over fourteen hundred other people, and that was not a large number; we probably should have met before now.

I ran into him at the Loxley Post office when I went in to get a book of stamps one Saturday morning after his release, and after I had initially followed him home from the farmers market. The Loxley Post office was a one-room L-shaped building; if somebody was there, you wouldn't miss him. Most folks received their mail at homes, so the post office wasn't a very active place. The businesses we had in the small town received service where your postman brought your mail directly to you, and found time to chat on most days. The business area of the town was so small that the postal carrier still walked the route. Starting at eight, he could be finished by eleven most mornings.

As I turned to the left to go through the glass door and into the counter area, which was smaller than my walk-in closet at home, I pulled on the door and ran chest first into Larry Cunningham. As my mouth fell open, he stood aside with an "excuse me" and a big smile. I acknowledged him with a slight nod and walked into the small space. The postmaster stood at the counter, leaning on one elbow and looking at the door Larry Cunningham just exited.

"Seems unreal, doesn't it?" he asked, as much to himself as me. "I can't understand it. Not on any level." He looked down and continued to process his paperwork. The postmaster shook his head, so deep in his thoughts that he seemed to forget I was even there.

I turned, still in shock, and looked out into the parking lot as the same blue Ford pulled out onto Front Street. From behind me I heard the postmaster say, "Something has got to be done about that guy." I'm sure that he was talking to himself and not to me. I'm sure he wasn't the only member of our community thinking the same thing. I just had no idea how to even respond to this.

"You got that right," I heard someone say, then realized it was me who had said it. I moved as if walking through thigh-high mud back to the counter to get my stamps. I couldn't remember what I needed or why I was there, but the postmaster didn't seem to be aware that I acted strangely. As I asked for a book of stamps, he looked over my shoulder and out the window. I knew that he was thinking the same thing I'd been thinking.

What can we do about this?

CHAPTER 18

▼

The second time I went to Larry Cunningham's house was a little more than a week later. I was returning from a weekend at the beach with Cora and my mother. The weather was getting a little cooler now, and the beach was less fun for a whole weekend for a teenager. Cora and my mother had decided to do some shopping on the trip home, so Cora rode with Mom, and they stopped at the outlet malls in Foley. The two of them loved to shop together; it was, in fact, the only thing they enjoyed doing together. My mother was a little too old to put my with the drama queen, Cora, most days.

I felt absolutely compelled to drive down that part of Highway 55 and take one more look at the Cunningham place. When I was about two miles from Larry's house, I realized what I was doing: scouting the property. Just a hundred yards before Larry's driveway was a red clay road that ran parallel to Larry's property. I noticed it the last time I had driven by the house, but I hadn't ventured down the road. This time, I turned on the red clay road just to take a look.

The road ran between Larry's property and a pecan orchard still farmed by the Alegrie family. Alegrie was also the current police officer for this small town. Since Larry's predecessors built this house, Larry's yard on both the north and the south side, had been allowed to grow up wild. With the woods in back of the house, the property was concealed on three sides. If I looked at the house from the highway, between the wooded area on two sides and the huge oak trees in the front yard, only a small corner of the house was visible.

I was scouting, taking mental notes as I turned onto the red clay road on the south side of Larry's property. I knew subconsciously what I was doing: checking out the way he lived, access to his property. I was a little concerned about why I couldn't let this whole thing go and get on with my life, but I didn't seem to be able to do that yet. I spent time thinking about Larry Cunningham when other things should have been much more important to me, like my job and my responsibilities to Cora.

About four hundred yards off the highway; I pulled off to the side of the dirt road and stopped my truck. I sat for a minute, just looking around and trying to assess the location. The road hadn't been traveled recently. Red clay will show marks in the clay when it's traveled, and I thought that if the road was traveled, it wasn't often. The pecans had been harvested for the year, and there was no other reason to come down this road It had been a rainy week, so the clay was slippery even with the heat of the day. Red Alabama clay feels like snow when it gets wet. You slip and slide just like you would in Maine in January. I had seen many folks "from away" who thought that the clay was just dirt, so it must behave like dirt. Not true. It wasn't, and the people who believed that, were the folks you saw in the roadside ditches during a rain storm. If you've ever seen *My Cousin Vinny*, you may remember the red Alabama clay scene. Hollywood got it right.

Getting out of the truck, I thought that this damn clay would ruin my white sneakers. Red Alabama clay was not only slippery, but the red would turn everything it touched into a lovely rust color when wet. There was actually a company that made shirts for tourists in Alabama by using the red clay to color shirts and they sold them for fifteen dollars apiece as Alabama Mud Shirts. I wished I would have thought that one up.

Being careful to stay on my feet, I closed the truck door and eased off the road and into the brush on the side of the road that led to the back of Larry's property.

"Damn it, I hope I don't see any snakes. I hate snakes," I said to myself as I walked into the woods toward Larry's back yard.

As a hunter, I had been in the woods all my life. I knew a couple of things about direction, and watching where you were, and remembering which way you had come. I also knew a thing or two about snakes, like always stepping on top of fallen logs, not over them because most snakes loved to lie on the side of logs. Stepping over the log and on the snake pissed them off.

Alabama had poisonous snakes of many varieties, and I hated them all because I was a chicken when it came to snakes. We had so many that the school system had a standard program about what to do if you were bitten by a snake, and what types of snakes to panic over once bit. My philosophy, which was not environmentally correct or remotely logical, was the only good snake, was a dead snake.

Slowly, I walked through the woods. I wasn't really sneaking but I was trying to be careful about the amount of noise I was making. This was just like deer hunting. You were busy watching your feet, making sure to watch for anything that might skitter toward your feet, and at the same time looking around for any large, hairy white-tails that you might scare up. White-tailed deer can lie just feet away from your path in the brush and until you step on them, they might not move. It was a toss-up as to who was more scared in that situation: the one-hundred-twenty-five-pound wild animal with horns or the one-hundred fifteen-pound silly girl hunter too surprised to remember she was the one carrying the gun. Carefully and quietly, I crept another hundred yards toward Larry's property.

I could see the rooftop of his house through the trees. I had found my feet now, and I moved forward in a crouch. I stopped and listened every couple of yards. From this position, I saw most of the long driveway and the rear of Larry's house. No truck in the drive was a good sign. It didn't appear that anybody was home. I hoped to do my scouting without being discovered. I took several more steps toward the tree line and the back yard to better my position.

The brick house sat in the middle of the yard but the driveway ended beyond the house. A carport/garage was open on all four sides where Larry must have parked just one truck. I was sure that the carport made it convenient for dropping things off and carrying items in the back door. There was no side door on the house and the back door was accessed by a large wooden deck. It appeared that the deck has been built within the last five years, and I remembered that Larry has only lived in this community for about that much time since he had returned to the area and the Lutheran Church.

When Larry was arrested, every fact about his life, including the house where many of the sexual assaults had happened, was front page news. Several stories mentioned that Larry spent several years away from the area, which gave the locals some comfort that he wasn't "one of us." It was funny how they had turned on him; he was a local hero one minute and a lowlife, perverted tourist the next.

The back yard lived up to everything that I had read in the papers about Larry's love of the outdoors. The yard was beautiful, well cared for, and obviously a green hand, instead of only a green thumb had been at work here. The fall color was coming in and most of the summer color was still healthy. He had an attention to detail that would be admirable if he wasn't so sick.

Rose beds with yellow, pinks and red blooms lined the back deck. I remembered reading that Larry had often taken roses to the mothers of the boys that he was molesting; the article had also stated that he grew his own roses. Crepe myrtles in full bloom framed both sides of the yard in pinks and whites, drooping gracefully over the perfect green Saint Augustine grass. The branches swayed with the breeze that I had not noticed or felt until now.

I wondered how much time Larry must have spent each year, planting and maintaining his secret garden. The newspaper articles reported the boys had spent time here in the back yard, working with Larry on the flowers. One year Larry started his garden and the boys had taken it on as a project, learning to maintain it and developing skills for growing things later in life.

On the back deck was a top-dollar Coleman gas grill with a tan wicker patio table and four chairs. The patio table had an umbrella with dark green and light pink stripes on it. I noticed that the light pink stripe matched the pink roses planted just under the railing of the deck. The windows along the back of the house all have window boxes in them with more pink pansies dripping over the edges of the boxes. Planters with various herbs occupied the four corners of the deck. The total effect was Hansel-and-Gretel-gingerbread-house cute. I guessed that made Larry the evil witch who ate children in the fairy tale. I shivered at this thought and looked up at the roof to see a chimney. Of course, nothing was coming out of the chimney, but I pictured the evil man shoving children in the fireplace like the evil witch had shoved children in the oven of her gingerbread house.

In the middle of the yard was an old pump house, sitting over the unused water well. These are not uncommon in this part of the country. Most of the homes built and passed down by farming families weren't close enough to city utilities to have city water. City water had been run down this part of the county road two years ago. Larry had found an alternative use for this pump house and painted it to match the larger version of his real house. It was like looking at Larry's house remade for small hobbits, complete with window boxes and a back deck. The only thing missing was the real flowers. Someone had painted the flowers in the window boxes on the small house to make it look like the boxes were planted year-round.

This scouting mission had taken longer than I had expected, and the sun began to fall out of the sky. I needed to get home before Cora and my mother ended their shopping trip. Working carefully back toward the truck, I thought about how normal Larry seemed on the surface. I once heard the saying. "He's a mile wide and an inch thick." Meaning that the guy was all surface, a laminate with no depth. Larry, on the other hand, was the exact opposite: he was miles deep and totally evil. His surface seemed so normal but under that surface was a scary being. I was scared for the local kids and especially those kids from his church. He had already manipulated those kids and their mothers. What, and who, would he do it to next? Something had to be done.

Obsessed is such an overused word. The dictionary says that it means "to haunt or trouble a mind." As I found my way back down the red clay road, through the woods and out of Larry's backyard, I truly understood what the word obsession meant. I was obsessed with stopping Larry from ever hurting another child.

On my fifth visit over four months, I went through the woods and up to his back yard where I'd noticed an old deer hunting stand in the woods to the right side of the house. I made my way over and looked up to see its condition.

Like most deer stands, it was made of wood with a ladder leading upward. Deer stands come in all shapes and sizes, but this one was approximately fifteen feet off the ground. The ladder, still in fair shape, led to a platform tucked protectively back in the branches of a large oak tree. The stand was no more than a three by three foot platform, strapped to the tree with a chain and bolts. The ladder appeared to be okay, and on my trip the month before, I had climbed up to see the view from fifteen feet up. I could see why someone had built that stand. It was convenient to the house and from up in the air, you could see deer trails throughout the woods below.

The woods were filled with oak trees and acorns, which kept the deer coming this close to an occupied house. The tree stand had been used originally as a bow hunting stand. Bow hunting required that you get much closer to the prey than when you used a rifle. Using a rifle this close to a house wasn't a good practice. Arrows have a much shorter range and are much more predictable that high-power rifle bullets. This stand was a perfect bow hunter's location. The woods were just enough cover for the hunter sitting in the stand to hide from the prey and also had enough visibility to get a good clear shot at the deer.

My prey, however, would be in the other direction, in a clear green back yard. It was the perfect plan. Larry would come to admire his landscaping prowess and it would be the perfect shot.

As I sat there in the stand, I considered what I was doing. I knew from watching TV that the police would look first for motive. Half of Baldwin County had good motive to kill this monster. However, the police would focus on the victims, their family members, or friends. I was none of the above. I was a spectator who had no more of a motive than anyone else who read the newspaper. As far as my motives went, I was way down the list of possible murderers. I was concerned for the people who truly had a motive, but I counted on them either having an alibi or the police not having enough proof to convict. Hell, they had Larry dead to rights, and he was walking around a free man.

I had also worked an alibi for myself. I would be on a conference call with twenty other managers as the killer struck. My office phone would be forwarded to a pre-paid cell phone. I would log into the call using an 800 number, and using a pass code that could easily be traced back to me, I would confirm that I was there during the roll call, put the phone on mute and stay on the line. My office was at the rear of the store. I could easily be filmed going into the office; there were plenty of cameras in the store to confirm that. But the cameras didn't cover the administrative offices in the store, and I could walk out the back of the store and into my car without being seen. It would appear from the cameras that I was in the office the whole time. So even if someone thought to check on me as a suspect, they would have to prove I wasn't at the office.

The bigger question that I asked myself repeatedly was why? What was making me do this crazy thing? Maybe it was the fact that I desperately wanted children and couldn't have my own. Maybe that had created some kind of deep need to protect children from people who didn't deserve them because I couldn't have them. I walked through Wal-Mart, looking at children with their mothers, wanting my own so badly. I had been so lucky to have Cora and my other foster children, but I despised the people who had abused these kids. I couldn't stop them all, but maybe I could stop this one. At the base of all these thoughts and emotions was that Larry shouldn't be allowed to get away with what he had done or be able to do it again.

On one previous occasion when I knew Larry was not home, I had taken the chance to step out of the woods and measure the distance between the back porch and the tree stand. It was an easy shot with a rifle, by any hunter's calculation.

Now it was just a matter of luck—where opportunity met good solid planning.

CHAPTER 19

▼

As Katie sat in the tree stand, she was as still as possible, alone in the silent woods. It was a beautiful afternoon; the temperature was eighty-two degrees with low humidity. It was a little warmer than usual for this time of year, and she felt calm and comfortable sitting in the woods. She looked over at the tree next to the stand and saw a bird's nest with small blue eggs in it. She wondered what lived there and where the occupants were now. Had they seen her and flown away, understanding that something bad was going to happen? As if in answer to the question, a large female blue jay landed in the nest only ten feet away. The bird turned and noticed a strange animal in the tree stand. She jumped from foot to foot, chirping at the stranger so close to her nest. Staying still didn't matter to wild birds in the woods; they still went crazy if something invaded their space. Mother blue jay now had a birdie fit, flapping her wings and screeching at the top of her lungs.

"Shut up, you crazy bird," Katie thought to herself, not moving a muscle.

This distraction almost caused Katie to miss Larry's truck pulling into the drive. She heard the truck crunching up the gravel under its tires. She sat there and tried not to move an inch. "Shit, shut up, bird!" she thought. Hearing the truck, the bird was alerted and flew off to safer territory.

Katie moved her head slowly toward the approaching truck, careful not to make enough movement for anyone to see her. Often, when deer hunting it wasn't the deer that you saw it was the movement. They were in natural camouflage, but the movement of the animal attracted attention. Katie moved her head a quarter inch at a time, careful to move slowly, so even the small movement would seem more like something in the breeze than someone in a tree. She wore her full camo, which made it very hard to see her in the tree.

Larry parked just a hundred yards away at the end of his driveway, next to the house. He was looking down at the floor board of the passenger seat at something, Katie could not see inside the car from here. Picking up a plastic bag from Wal-Mart, Larry got out of the truck, swinging both legs out of the side of the truck and, then jumping down on the gravel drive. He reached into the back bed of the truck for a large bag of Over and Out Fire Ant Killer.

Larry moved toward the back yard and closer to Katie in the tree stand. Katie was close enough to be able to hear him now; Larry was humming a hymn under his breath. She knew that song but couldn't place it yet. "The Church in the Wildwood," that was the name of the song. Katie slowly moved only one finger toward the safety switch. With no more motion than the fire ant carrying a load five times his size, Katie clicked off the safety on her gun.

Larry moved to the side of the house and dumped the Over and Out next to the green spreader sitting next to the house. He was still humming and he moved over to the deck. The Wal-Mart bag in his right hand went onto the back porch then he moved into the yard with the determined look of a man searching for something. Larry walked around the yard, looking at the ground, and Katie guessed that Larry was locating the ant beds.

Just like the deer that doesn't sense the danger and believed he was safe, Larry moved away from the safety of the house and out into the wide open back yard. "Damn ants," Larry said to no one at all. As he walked from ant bed to ant bed checking them out, Katie held her breath as her prey moved closer. Katie slowly raised the gun as her prey comes within seventy yards of the stand. The prey wasn't facing Katie, but stood sideways to her stand. She waited just like she'd been taught by her father, waited for the best shot possible. She had spent too much time planning this moment to get in a hurry now.

Larry stopped at the old pump house in the back yard and bent over to look at what the ants have built around the base of the house. As he stood up straight, he turned just thirty degrees, giving Katie a clear view of the chest shot she needed. He stood still, hands on hips, just sixty-five yards away. It was an easy shot with a .308 rifle and a six-by-nine Leopold scope both well maintained and recently sighted in at the rifle range.

Katie moved the scope up to check the face of the animal she was about to kill, one more time to check the identity of the prey. She took another small breath and held it. She slowly she tightened her grip on the trigger.

When deer hunting, it was always a good idea to check the prey with your own eyes, but often you aren't close enough to the kill to tell with the naked eye what you have, so you had to use the scope to check out the animal. A doe standing in front of a tree with limbs right behind her could look like a buck, with the limbs appearing to be horns on her bare head. This was why Katie had been taught to look through the scope at the prey and confirm what she had before she pulled the trigger.

In this situation, the confirmation was even more vital. She convinced herself that it was just a target, an animal that needed to be put down. It wasn't another human being, not a man with a family and friends. Her prey was a sick and deadly animal that needed to be put out of his misery.

She made sure she had the scope perfectly positioned on his chest so the shot would have the maximum effect. The good thing about a .308 for deer hunting was that it had a big punch. It would generally drop the deer where it stood. Katie had hunted for years with a .243, but her dad suggested that if she wanted to kill her deer and not have to track them a long way in the woods, a "big boy gun" like a .270 or .308 was necessary. She had been hunting with this .308 for seven years. She purchased the gun from the L.L. Bean store, before it was required to register guns. It was going to be hard to trace, in any circumstance, but the age and location of the purchase added a little more comfort to Katie's situation.

The gun went off, as if by magic, and her eyes closed by reflex. It was only for one second, but in hunting, you never knew what you would see when you opened your eyes again. She always wanted to see her kill on the ground, exactly where he was standing before you pulled the trigger. In deer hunting, it didn't always work that way. Often times, they ran. This was not the case with Larry Cunningham.

Katie was lucky today. Her prey lay right were he stood just moments ago. Katie slowly let out her breath and lowered the gun to a resting position in her lap. Her arms had strained from holding the gun up, waiting for a good shot, and looking through the scope. She shook both arms out while keeping her eyes on the kill in the middle of the yard the whole time, making sure that he was not moving.

Nothing was moving; it appeared to be a clean kill. She didn't want to think what would have happened if she had missed or if the shot hadn't instantly killed him. It seemed like hours passed, but it was only moments and she sat still again, watching the kill and the front of the house to make sure that no one was coming up the drive. She knew that she was safe for now, but she also understood that getting out of there fairly quickly was a good idea.

She has assessed the situation well, planned the kill and the retreat. The closest neighbor wasn't at home this evening but even if they were, they wouldn't have thought twice about the sound of a single gunshot this time of year. In these parts, with dove hunting and deer hunting and killing coyotes, neighbors would take a single gun shot in stride. This was the country; everyone had a gun and used those guns often.

Slowly, Katie put her gun over her shoulder and climbed out of her borrowed tree stand. The gun strap pulled tightly against her body; she climbed hand over hand down the old wooden steps. She got three steps down and remembered to go back up to get the spent cartridge from the gun. Not a good thing to leave lying around. She climbed the rest of the way out of the stand, and walked slowly over to the body lying in the middle of a peaceful back yard, next to a pump house that had not been in service since they put in city water and sewer years ago.

She took a good hard look at the body of Larry Cunningham. She checked to make sure that he was dead by placing the barrel of the gun to his open eye. Just for good measure, she put her boot on his side and pushed a little to see if she got a reaction. She got nothing. She turned and walked away from what she had done, mission complete, plan executed.

CHAPTER 20

$$\blacktriangledown$$

For Wes Harmon, it was another beautiful day. His phone had rung first thing that morning before he was out of the shower calling him to another crime scene. As he drove down Highway 55, listening to the police radio, he heard an update on his police radio about a possible shooting victim. They had just found the body yesterday he heard but it was just background noise for him. First and foremost on his mind, was what Debbie, his soon-to-be ex-wife had said this morning before she hung up the phone on him.

Debbie had walked out on Wes, taking his two girls, ages four and six, with her to her mother's house. This was not a new thing for him; a previous wife had walked out years ago and took his other two girls with her. Wes had called this morning to talk Debbie into coming home one more time. He thought that this time they would be able to work it out. She was upset but he knew that he could talk his way through it, just one more time. Over the past couple of days, their discussions had turned into begging on his part.

"But, baby, this is fixable. Now I know your issues, now I understand what you need. I can fix all of this. No problem!" Wes said. Wes was not a man who would plead like this, especially with a woman. He was generally a confident man; he had negotiated with criminals for years. In law enforcement, he had to be a master at communication and he felt that he was pretty good at it. Hell, he had the gun at his side every day; what did he have to worry about? Unfortunately, his ex-wives never seemed to care how good he was at his job; they cared about things like being home for dinner and remembering the kid's birthdays. These were things that he was never good at.

When he called, the only answer he got this time was a heavy sigh from the other end of the phone from his ex-wife was the only answer he got this time. Debbie was only forty-five miles away at her mom's house in Pensacola. She had been gone this time for two weeks, but as far as Wes was concerned, she could have been living on the moon for the last hundred years. He missed her and the girls. This wasn't the first phone call like this one he had made during their marriage. Debbie had left him and taken the girls away before, but he had always been able to get her back. Wes had progressed from one desperate phone call a day to several. Most of the calls he made were after nine o'clock when the kids would have been in bed and Debbie would have been able to talk. That time of night was when he was the loneliest and needed her the most.

Even though she had been doing nothing but fussing and yelling for over a year, he missed their relationship. She had begged, threatened, made promises, cried and pleaded for the whole time they had been together, but it took Wes coming home two weeks ago to the empty house for him to listen to what she was really saying.

"Wes, you don't get it. These are not 'my issues'. You're a drunk!" Debbie stated one night, more calmly than Wes thought she was capable for the past year. Everything that came out of her mouth had led up to this minute. The difference was she didn't sound mad anymore. Wes didn't like how she had sounded; she sounded relieved. And it hit him that the relief might be that she didn't have to deal with him any longer. That was his worst nightmare; he knew that when they were yelling at you, they still cared. When a woman stopped yelling and crying, it meant that she was over you and ready to go on with her life. Wes didn't think that he could take another divorce.

"Baby, I'll stop drinking. You won't see me drink ever again. I swear. That's the easy part. See, I hear you and it's done. Over. Finished." He didn't mention the twelve pack of Coors Light that he had drunk last night after the third pleading phone call to Florida. Wes hated the tone in his voice; the pleading was gone. He was whining now. How could he handle a career in law enforcement for twenty years but had been married three times before his fortieth birthday? Why was he such a screw-up when it came to relationships? They always seemed to love him to distraction at the beginning. Heaven knew, he didn't change a thing.

"That's great, Wes. Good luck!" And with that Debbie hung up the phone, just hung up the phone.

What was that all about? Hell, he was serious. He would do it. The thought of being divorced four times was not an option. He had to save this. Read the headlines "Police officer divorced four times", now there is a phenomenon. Somebody, quick call Ripley's Believe it or Not. When Wes thought about all the police officers he knew; very few had only been married once. For a group of people who were by trade cynical, they seemed to believe in trying their hands at love over and over again. Wes, even after three failed marriages, believed that this one should have worked.

As he crossed over highway 104 and continued south to the crime scene, he knew that it is just a matter of proving to Debbie that he could stay sober. She just needed to cool off, and then she would be back in no time. This was just a hiccup in their relationship. He needed to put his mind on his work: the body that he was going to see.

It took just a minute to see the emergency lights from the county, state and local law enforcement and rescue workers to know where he was going. Noticing that the driveway was gravel and was packed with other agency cars, Wes parked on the grass of the front yard and walked up the driveway and into the back yard. It didn't take long to see that this was a full-fledged, all-out, grade A mess. There were more cops in this back yard than in downtown Mobile on Mardi Gras. A quick look around and he saw every uniform color and type in the lower part of the State. "Good Lord, this is going to be a mess," he mumbled to himself.

Wes had been a member of the Homicide Task Force since it had started five years ago in the county. The Task Force was Baldwin County's way to maximize the opportunities to solve crimes that law enforcement agencies throughout the state had by improving communication with one another. Several cases had not gone as well as they should have in Alabama because the different agencies weren't set up to communicate with one another. The Governor worked with all the agencies and funded the Task Force statewide. Anytime there was a questionable death, the Task Force would be called to review the evidence and make recommendations, if not first then at least second. Wes represented the sheriff's department. The point was to make sure that everyone had all the knowledge and expertise of the other departments: local, county and state. Once, the federal guys had even gotten into the fray, but that was the exception, not the rule. Wes figured the Federal guys must be bored; hell, nothing interesting ever happened around here except for the drugs that seemed to be everywhere in this part of the state, and they weren't interested in recreational drugs, so they had a lot of down time on their hands.

"Hey, Wes! What's up?" said a twenty-one-year-old kid. Stevie Miller worked for the Silverhill Police Department. This particular back yard sat just outside the town limits of Silverhill, but anything for a little entertainment, so these guys showed up.

"Not much, Stevie. How's your dad handling Dale Jr. being number one in the point's race?" Steve's father was a huge NASCAR fan.

"Happy as a pig in shit, Sir. This is our year, Man! Our year!" hollered Stevie. He held up his thumb and pinky in a classic surfer wave.

Wes passed him by. A group of uniformed officers stood around what looked like a pump house, or maybe a dog house, in the back yard.

Wes had been in law enforcement in one capacity or another all his life. As Wes walked up to the officers in the Cunningham back yard, he thought that he'd been at this job a long time, and he really needed a vacation soon. He noted he knew everyone, shaking hands as he made his way through the crowd. There were two patrolmen from the City of Silverhill and the chief of police. Silverhill was a small force with only seven patrolmen and one Sergeant. The police chief was even part-time. It would be the sheriff's department that took the lead on this show.

"Hey, Wes," said Silverhill Chief of Police Jody Alegrie. "I guess this isn't a big surprise. Probably could have called it the day they let him out of jail. This situation was just a matter of when and how."

Wes didn't answer but moved around to the body laying face down on the ground. It lay with one hand out straight and the other under the body. The outstretched hand was still holding a bag of Over and Out, used to kill fire ants. Wes made a note to himself that he needed to remember to get some for his own yard; he always had a fire ant problem this time of year. Wes noticed that the clothes and the body had been out in the weather for some time. This was not a very fresh body.

Both legs were together as if he had just lain down to get some sun or maybe was putting out ant killer and decided to take a little nap. The smell coming from the body was like rotten eggs but mellower. The minimal smell probably had something to do with the amount of time he had been dead and the fact that he was outside.

"How long has he been this way?" Wes asked, turning to Hoss Mackay, the county coroner.

"I'm guessing five to seven days," said Hoss, a barrel-chested guy who had been county coroner for all his adult life. Hoss was the father of two boys and they would probably some day work for the coroner's office, too.

"What happened to his ankle?" asked a deputy. He bent over, looking at the piece of missing ankle that showed between the pants leg and shoe, which was still on the mangled foot.

"I'd guess that it was probably a coyote or a bobcat, this time of year," answered the Coroner. A deputy standing next to Wes looked quickly up from the body, turned around and threw up his breakfast on the ground not ten feet from the body. That drew a round of laughs from the rest of the officers.

"Is it Cunningham?" asked Wes. He couldn't see the face but was feeling sure that it was.

"That's what the license in his back pocket says," answered Chief Alegrie. "Damn, hasn't been a killin' in Silverhill in twenty-seven years."

"Yeah, there was," said another officer, Alex. He was off duty, but couldn't pass up the excitement and showed up on his day off. He was a senior officer for Silverhill. Everyone turned from the body to look to him for an answer. "Remember old lady Warner shot her husband when she found out he was sleeping with that cute little barmaid at *Fish and Steak* in Loxley? Killed him dead." Alex added. Southerners were notorious for saying things like "Killed him dead." As if there is another way to kill them, other than dead.

"That wasn't no killin'! That was putting a low-life drunk dog out of his misery. That was a justifiable shooting" said Hoss, making everyone laugh. "Hell, I oughta know. Guy was my second cousin on my mother's side."

"Same as this one if you ask me. Justifiable as they come. Same as this one," said the chief under his breath. The chief turned away from the body and spit on the ground.

Wes took all of this in but looked off into the distance, toward the woods. "Any idea about the weapon or the direction of the shot, Hoss?" asked Wes looking back over his shoulder at the woods beyond the back yard.

"From the looks of it, we got a rifle, high power, either a .308 or maybe .270. From the shot and the blood pattern, shot came from the woods." Hoss turning to look in the same direction as Wes "Shot came from over there in the woods," Hoss pointed off into the woods, directly behind the pump house and the body.

"Okay, guys, enough standing around staring at his butt," said the chief. "This ain't Sammy's and he ain't any of you guys type anyway. And his ass ain't that noteworthy laying there. Why don't we all do a little police work, and let's look around for some clues? See if we can't at least pretend to care about finding out who did this. What y'all think? And be careful. Whether he deserved it or not, we still got a crime scene here. Be alert. Watch your feet and where you're putting them."

The officers moved off in different directions. It was the same routine with any crime scene: preserve the evidence and look for the explanation for what happened. Make sure you kept your eyes open, not only for what was there but for what wasn't there. Plastic bags came out and everybody started marking and bagging the crime scene.

Wes was miles ahead of the group. He moved directly toward the woods. He walked along the tree line, looking for a path through the woods. He sighted in a direct path from the body and moved to the right. There seemed to be a slight path right there through the trees, not beaten down, but enough to recognize that somebody had walked through these trees recently.

Wes pushed through the bushes and into the woods along what looked like the path. He looked up into the trees and saw an old hunting ladder stand. Wes walked to the bottom of the hunting ladder and looked up directly at the bottom of the platform. It wasn't much but it could still hold somebody. Wes moved into the woods and put his hands on both sides of the ladder. He looked up at the rotten wood platform, gave the ladder a little shake to test it to see if it was solid, then climbed up the first couple of rungs. He shook the ladder again while standing on the third step just to make sure that it would hold him and kept climbing up.

When Wes put a knee on the platform to pull himself up, a loud crack made him grab the tree. The top rung of the ladder broke completely in two and fell to the ground fifteen feet below. "Damn," he said to himself.

He turned, got his butt under him, and got comfortable on the platform. Feeling unsure that the platform wasn't going to fall, he looked into the woods and made himself comfortable on the seat. If he turned a quarter to the right, and leaned just a little around the tree, he was completely invisible to anyone looking, but he could see everyone in the back yard including the body of Larry Cunningham. He estimated the distance and looked at the tree limbs for any marks. He found a small rub on the tree limb and knew that this was where the killer balanced the gun to steady his shot.

"Not a hard shot. Definitely not a hard shot for a seasoned shooter." Wes pulled up an imaginary rifle and leveled it at the coroner who was standing over the body. That would have been the shot the hunter saw when Larry Cunningham was still standing on his own feet. "Bang," Wes said, pulling the imaginary trigger.

Getting down from the tree was a little more difficult; starting without the top rung on the ladder was tricky. Once back on the ground, Wes looked over the area for any signs of footprints. Nothing. The rain over the last several days had washed away any sign of foot traffic. The ground beneath the stand was all oak leaves and an inch and a half of moss. Nothing would leave a track in this stuff for very long, he thought.

As Wes walked back into the yard, the chief saw the look of discovery on Wes's face. "What ya think? You find something."

"Shot came from that old deer stand over there. There are marks on the tree limbs where the shooter used the branches for a balance. The path into the woods is barely there at this point, which means that it probably wasn't used much, but it was used recently. I think what happened was, the shooter climbed up there and sat to wait on our low life here to come home. Everybody that knew this jerk understood that he loved his yard and his pretty flowers, thanks to the newspaper articles about his personal habits.

"Whoever pulled the trigger knew what they are doing. The shot is a clean kill shot, hitting him in the bottom part of the heart. You can tell by looking at the angle of the entrance wound and the angle of the exit wound. The gun is probably a hunting rifle and with a decent scope on it; anybody who knew how to load a gun could have made that shot. The scope would also mean that whoever pulled the trigger knew what, and who, they were shooting. No chance that it was a mistake. Larry never saw it coming. I could see you guys from up there but my bet is that you wouldn't see me unless you were looking real close. Add a camo shirt and hat, maybe some face cover and you'd never see me," explained Wes.

"With a little planning and good timing, this guy never had a chance," added one of the state cops.

"The timing works for what we think, too. We found a receipt for the Over and Out in his truck from the Wal-Mart. Shows he was in the Foley store at 2:35 p.m., five days ago. We talked to his brother and the last time he saw Larry was last Wednesday, and that's where he was headed," the chief said. "Sounds like somebody was waiting for him when he came home."

"Yep. Sounds like," Wes agreed, moving toward the house and the back deck. The chief and Wes stepped over the body like it was a discarded piece of trash, and stepped onto the back porch.

As they turned and looked back over the yard, the EMTs moved across the back yard with the stretcher. Under the direction of Hoss, the EMTs moved the stretcher closer to the body, time to move the body to the shop. When the two EMTs were correctly set, one EMT grabbed the shoulders and one grabbed the legs. Another officer hooked both hands into Larry's belt, and they rolled Larry into the black body bag lying on the ground next to the body. After Larry was zipped up, they all three grabbed the black bag and pushed it onto the stretcher.

"Piece-a-shit," said the younger of the two EMTs as they lift the bag.

"What did you say?" asked Hoss, turning back toward them. "Even the dead deserve respect young man."

"Not this one, Hoss. One of them kids was my friend's son and I worked right beside this guy at the Fire Department as a volunteer. The kid was only seven. Damn it." said the EMT, looking first at his hands and then at the body bag. "We should just dump this bag of garbage off at the landfill."

Having heard the exchange, all the officers, EMTs and onlookers stood watching in stunned silence.

If there were two things everyone in the law enforcement community knew about Hoss Mackay, one was that he was respectful of all his clients, regardless of how they had lived. The other was that you didn't ever want his temper directed at you. Hoss didn't allow any of his staff to cut corners just because someone was a criminal. Leaders in the community got the same high quality treatment in his morgue as the lowest form of life. Hoss was about respect—alive or dead.

Hoss looked at the kid; the kid looked at Hoss with anger in his young eyes. "Get him to my office, boys." Hoss understood that the kid's heart was in the right place and no more suffering was necessary. It was a little hard to argue with the kid on this one. Cunningham was a known child molester, and he understood that this EMT was voicing the feelings that a large part of community had voiced when Larry was let loose. Hoss slapped the kid on the back and turned to walk to the back porch.

"We're going to get a lot of that," Alegrie said, overhearing the exchange between the EMT and the coroner. "People are going to react to this shooting like nothing else. I think folks are actually going to be happy he isn't around anymore." The chief looked down at his boots. "I know I am."

"Maybe," Wes said. He knew the chief was right about his feelings and thought about the group of mothers: Jennifer, Jamie and the others.

"I can't say that I'm not a little tickled that the guy isn't going to be living in my neighborhood. Hell, my kids went to school with those boys. Don't really know what I'd do if anybody ever got after my kids that way," the chief said, more to himself than anyone. "Maybe I'd get out my gun, too."

"Enough. You want to get reelected, you'll think that but won't let it come out of your mouth," Hoss said as he walked up. "The press is out front and they're asking for both of you," Hoss turned to walk away and added with a smile, "Oh, and somebody said David Whitman is here too!" He laughed and kept walking toward his car. Hoss wasn't a fan of the DA, but you would never get him to say it in public.

"Let the games begin," Chief Alegrie said, pushing Wes ahead of him and off the porch toward the front yard and the press.

CHAPTER 21

▼

Wes pulled up to the Kollman house just before six that night. He had hoped to arrive before Jennifer had seen the nightly news. The DA and the press had promised a low-key piece on the murder of Larry Cunningham. But tomorrow, the leash came off, and the whole thing was fair game. Law enforcement just wanted a little time to ask some questions and see what they could find out before the circus that would surround this murder started.

"Just a minute," came a voice from inside the house when Wes rang the door bell. Wes shifted from foot to foot like a high school boy picking up his date for the prom. He liked Jennifer; he liked all the mothers for that matter. He remembered them sitting in the courtroom when Larry was released. He thought that they looked like scared chickens, all huddled up together in the back of the room. There was no way to make them understand what had happened that day, and he hoped that none of them had anything to do with Larry lying in the morgue right now.

"Yes?" called Jennifer, surprised when she opened the door and saw it was Wes. Jennifer and Wes's current wife, soon to be ex-wife, had known each other since Jennifer moved back to town. They had spent time at school functions, kid's sports functions, PTA meetings. She knew from the general gossip that Wes and Debbie's separation had been coming for a while. Everyone knew it was coming except Wes. She felt sorry for him; he was the only one who hadn't realized that Debbie had mentally divorced him ages ago.

"Wes, good to see you," said Jennifer, not really meaning it. Jennifer had held Wes responsible for Larry being released from jail. He had been their primary point of contact throughout the investigation. He had been the first person they had reported the information to and they had expected that he would see it through to the end. The DA's office had said that it had nothing to do with the police but Jennifer and the other ladies hadn't believed it for a minute. The DA was pointing the finger at the police and the police were pointing the finger at the DA's office. Wes showing up at dinner time was unexpected and unwanted. Jennifer really liked her time alone at dinner with Jacob, and Wes showing up right now was a distraction. Oh well, what was one more pair of feet under the table? She had plenty for all three of them. "Come on in. I've got dinner about half out of the oven. You hungry?" She headed back toward the kitchen.

Wes stepped into the foyer and closed the door behind him. "I'm not really hungry, Jen, but I do need to speak with you if you've got a minute." He followed her into the kitchen. When he stepped through the doorway she already has a spoonful of something that smelled like heaven ready for him.

She held the spoon to his mouth and her other hand under the spoon to keep it from dripping on the floor. "Taste this." She put the spoon in his mouth before he could say no thanks.

What melted in his mouth was pure heaven. Wes's stomach rumbled, wanting more.

"Crab melt for dinner," she told him as she turned to lower the heat on the stove. "Got the recipe from LuLu's Restaurant in Gulf Shores; isn't it great? I picked out the crabs with mom just last week at the beach house. I've been to Lulu's about five times trying to figure out what's in their crab melt and I think I've finally figured it out. This is really pretty easy to make once you get the spices right."

Wes's stomach rumbled again as he took another sniff and looked in the pan she was stirring. "Maybe I am a little hungry," he said, looking over her shoulder. "I can't remember if I had lunch today, or breakfast this morning."

"Lord bless ya, Wes. You've got to eat." Jennifer spooned a mixture of crab meat, cheese, green onions and spices onto bread dipped in olive oil. "Jacob, dinner!" she called up the stairs, moving three plates to the table.

Wes heard footsteps running down the stairs, and Jacob slid into his place at the table. "Hey, Mr. Harmon. What you doing here?" Jacob asked, not waiting for the answer. He grabbed his plate and spooned the crabmeat mixture over the top of the bread.

"Having dinner. Now say grace, Jacob," ordered his mother.

Wes decided to keep things light for dinner conversation and asked questions about Jacob's school and Jennifer's job. Wes and Jacob had a fun conversation about who would have the better football season: Alabama or Auburn. Jacob, who had always been a little too fond of cop shows on TV, wanted to hear stories about cops and bad guys. Once Jacob and Wes finished their dinner, Jennifer picked up the plates and began to load the dishwasher.

"You're done, young man. Leave Wes and I alone, and you can watch TV for a little while before bedtime." Jennifer finished loading the dishwasher and wiped her hands on the dishtowel hanging from the handle on the fridge.

"Great dinner, Mom, thanks. Good to see you, Wes. Come back again, okay?" Jacob ran back upstairs to his room.

Jennifer finished clearing the rest of the table and put away the leftovers. Wes moved to help, but Jennifer said, "Stay put, Wes. You're not fooling anybody around here. My crab melt sandwiches are good but they aren't that good. I can tell you've got something to say, and this will go a lot quicker with only one person in this small kitchen." She moved between the table and the counter with speed and efficiency.

When the last pan was done and put away, Wes leaned back in the chair and took a deep breath. "Jen, I've got some information about Larry Cunningham. It won't hit the news until tomorrow morning. We've got the DA on our side for once but as of 6:00 a.m., it will be out there." Wes said all of this to Jennifer without ever breaking eye contact with her.

"He did it again, didn't he?" she whispered looking toward the stairs and Jacob's closed door. Jennifer's hand went to cover her mouth like she might scream. "Oh, my God, no." Jennifer moved around the kitchen counter and sat down hard at the table. "Who was it this time?"

"No, Jen, no. That's not it at all." Wes took her hand across the table. "Not at all. Larry didn't do anything. Look, what I'm trying to say—and messing up really bad—is that Larry Cunningham is dead. Sorry to be so direct but Larry was shot in his back yard a few days ago. We found the body today, this afternoon." He sat and looked at Jennifer.

She didn't say a word and sat still. She had her hand over her mouth and all he could see was her eyes.

He couldn't tell what she was thinking. "Jen? You okay."

"What?" said Jennifer through her hands. She looked at Wes as if he has just told her that Ed McMahon was at the front door with the million-dollar check. "What did you say?" She moved her hand away; she was smiling.

"Larry Cunningham was shot to death in his back yard. We discovered the body this afternoon," Wes repeated. "We think that it must have been somebody that was involved with the incidents against the kids. We're afraid that it may have been planned for a while."

"Larry Cunningham?" Jennifer repeated, as if she knew that she should remember the name, but just couldn't figure out who Larry Cunningham was. "Larry Cunningham is dead?"

At a loss for what to say next, Wes tried again. "You haven't seen it on the news because, for once, Whitman agreed that he would give us a little time to investigate before it goes public. Once things like this get out, it's harder to get information from someone who may be involved or have knowledge of the incident."

"He was shot? In his back yard?" asked Jennifer, putting her face in her hands.

"I thought I should get to you first. I wanted the news to come from me, not the TV," said Wes.

Jennifer had her face in her hands and he couldn't see the expression on her face. Her head was down and Wes noticed that her shoulders were shaking.

"Shit." he thought. "I hate when chicks cry." As he reached over to put his hand on her shoulder, the shaking got worse.

"Jen, it's okay." He stopped dead when she looked up with the huge grin, bigger than he had ever seen on her face before.

She began laughing—it was a giggle at first, then an out-and-out belly laugh. Here was a professional woman, a mother who had been through a great deal with her divorce and raising a son alone. Jennifer was a woman who was very conservative and reserved. Jennifer got up from the table and danced around the breakfast bar and into the kitchen, in a disco dance from the late 70s. She continued to laugh out loud.

"Praise God, Praise God," yelled Jennifer, between the laughter. With hands in the air above her head, she looked at the ceiling in the kitchen but saw something way beyond that. She looked to Wes like one of the cast members on one of those religious shows that aired late at night, the ones where everybody in the audience was waving hands in the air and singing hymns.

"J-U-S-T-I-C-E, that is what it means to me," she sang to the old Aretha Franklin tune for *Respect.* Jennifer danced around the kitchen in bare feet, alternately singing and yelling, "Praise God! Thank you Jesus!"

A concerned Jacob looked down the stairs to see what all the noise was about. He was so thrilled to hear his mom happy that her being totally freaky didn't even embarrass him in front of Wes. Jacob came into the room and smiled at his crazy mom; this was the happiest he has seen her look in months, maybe years. He laughed with her and at her.

"What's up, Mom?" Jacob asked from the door. "You were drinking or something? You finally lost your mind?"

"No, baby," she said. She grabbed Jacob and twirled him like a ballroom dancer. "Justice and the wrath of God have found Larry Cunningham." She sang one more verse of her version of *Respect*.

She let go of Jacob to dance by herself. Jacob stood, mouth open, staring at his mom like she had lost her mind.

Jennifer continued to dance around Jacob. He stood in the middle of the kitchen floor and looked at his mother and Wes who still sat at the kitchen table. Jennifer had stopped singing but still hummed the *Respect* tune.

"Larry Cunningham's body was found today in his back yard. He'd been shot in the heart," said Wes, looking at the boy for a reaction. "Jen, I need to ask you if you know anything about Larry Cunningham being shot."

This question stopped Jennifer. Jennifer stopped humming, stopped dancing, and stared at Wes as if he has asked the most perplexing question ever.

"What, you think my mom shot Larry?" questioned Jacob.

"I didn't say that, Jacob." Wes spoke very low and calmly. "I'm just asking if anybody may have said anything that may be of help in the investigation." He looked down at his shoe as if it were the most interesting shoe ever. "Sometimes people make comments that don't seem important at the time but later, something happens and, you know, the innocent comment wasn't so innocent after all." He looked up. "You know whatever you say I'll make sure it's kept confidential as best I can."

Jennifer crossed over to the table faster than Wes would have thought possible. She leaned on the table with both palms on the flat hardwood, and looked directly at Wes. The intensity of her look kept Wes quiet.

"Look, Officer Harmon." She said his name like it tasted bad in her mouth "I'll be straight up with you. And I want it to be on the record. I didn't kill that son of a bitch. I don't know who killed that slime, but if I could have, you bet your ass, I would have pulled the trigger." Wes looked down at her hand on the table were her fists turned white from the pressure that her rage was causing.

"I'm glad that he's dead. May God forgive me later. I am overjoyed that somebody killed him. Did I talk or think about killing him? You're damn right I did. We all did. More than once," said Jennifer, not moving her eyes from Wes's eyes. "I hope the bastard rots in Dante's fourth level of hell! My only problem is that he didn't suffer enough. Maybe Satan can take care of that."

"Mom, no." Jacob took a step toward his mom. He worried that she might say too much. He had never seen her so angry in his life.

"Larry Cunningham should have suffered for what he did to my son. I trusted you to make him suffer by putting him in jail. I was the one who told everybody we needed to go to you and report what we knew." With this, she stabbed her finger into his chest. "I was the one who told everyone that justice would be done, and that the authorities would take care of it." She started to cry and Jacob moved to her side and put his hand on her arm. She wouldn't take her palms off the table and inched closer to Wes with each sentence.

"I thought you could handle this problem, Wes." She leaned in; close only inches from his face. "I was wrong. You didn't handle it, did you? And that monster got out and went on with his life. To work in his garden and he even came back to the church. Did you hear about that happy Sunday morning, Wes? Then we all had to change and go to another church because we couldn't stand to see him on Sunday." Jennifer cried and Jacob started to cry.

"Truth be told, if I had a gun and knew how to use it? Yes. I would gladly have pulled the trigger. Gladly." Jennifer yelled. "Whoever did kill him doesn't deserve to be punished; he deserves a big fat medal. So if you find him, remember, you should thank him for doing your job! Which is to protect our children!"

"Mom, please," Jacob cried. "Calm down. It's not Mr. Wes's fault, it's that judge's fault. He and that DA guy were the ones that let Larry out. That's what everybody is saying at school. I heard two teachers talking about it at break. They said that the police had done what they could, and it was Mr. Whitman's fault."

Jennifer didn't hear a word of what Jacob was saying. She still leaned over the table, just inches from Wes's face. She seemed to remember herself and stood up straight and brushed imaginary dust off her jeans. She looked down at Wes as if she wasn't sure why he was still there. Jennifer turned to her son and noticed him for the first time in several minutes. She moved protectively in front of her son and pushed him behind her. She turned to look at Wes.

"Get out of my house. You're not welcome here ever again," Jennifer whispered, trying to get her temper under control. "Just think of this house as one of your ex-wives' houses. You should be used to not being welcome in good women's houses; you've been kicked out of enough of them.

Wes stood up and moved toward the door.

"Have a drink, Wes, it might clear your thinking," she said just before he walked out the door.

CHAPTER 22

▼

I woke up the next morning and everything seemed strangely normal. Things were the same today as yesterday, at least outwardly. I went back to work as if nothing happened. I was able to justify it all in my mind by saying that I had just been on a little hunting trip. This time, the kill was a little different, it was just a different kind of game.

"Katie, we have a customer at the Returns register who wants to speak to a Manager," said Miss Martha when I picked my phone in my office a couple of hours into my day.

"I'll be right there." It was going to be just another day in retail. I always hated these calls because the public basically sucks. People who were otherwise kind people, who loved their children and their mothers, who went to church on Sunday and bought Girl Scout cookies at their front doors, not because they needed them but because they still believed in the value of kids learning community service, these same people were complete and total jerks when dealing with retail sales workers.

Retail, which was just one step above food and beverage as a career, was tough. The general public was pissed off about life, and they were looking for someone to take it out on. Working in retail, they figured you were too stupid to get a job in banking or teaching, so you were fair game for their insults and abuse. They don't know that both of those professions paid less than working for most big box retailers. They thought speaking to you as if you personally caused the blade on their lawn mower to break was appropriate.

I have one rule for my associates. "I get paid more than you do, so I'll take the shit, not you." I have only one rule for myself. "I'll do anything to help the customer until they cuss at me or attack me verbally or personally." That was where I drew my line. Step over that line and I walked away like you just vanished into thin air, and I become completely deaf.

As I walked through the store to the returns register, my mind was on the fifty things I needed to get done today and the seventeen year old Cora at home. My mind clicked through the list: First, check on training metrics for the month; we needed to be at 80 percent before the next week if we were going to be 100 percent by end of month. Second, what to do about the drug testing facility that wasn't checking picture IDs before drug testing our applicants. How did they know that the person taking the drug test was the person standing before them if they didn't look at the ID? Third, where were the ninety-day reviews for the associates that were due Friday? I had one supervisor that couldn't get reviews done on time no matter who asked for them. My fourth concern was why Cora was screaming over the phone at her boyfriend *again* last night. I understood that they were both young, and that young love was dramatic love, but good grief, they needed to give the drama a break. And fifth, when would that great-looking district loss prevention guy be back in the store again? God, was he gorgeous.

"Hey, darlin'!" said a man who looked to be about sixty-five-years-old wearing candy-apple red polyester shorts and a matching red cotton sleeveless T-shirt. My God, I had never seen anybody off the golf course that was dressed so badly. Coming out of the bottom of these horrendous red shorts were the whitest chicken legs I had ever seen. On the ends of those white legs, he wore brown Jesus sandals.

I had never seen this guy before in my life, but he held out his arms like he expected a hug from me. I stopped about six feet away from him to keep this from happening. He got a hurt expression on his face like I left him hanging.

"Hi, I'm Katie Race," I said, putting out my hand for him to shake. He looked down at my outstretched hand, which he wouldn't shake, and his very light comb-over fell into his eyes. I looked at a bald head, freckled with age spots. Good Lord, what does this jackass want? I thought but what I said was, "How may I help you?"

He looked up and brushed the Donald Trump comb-over back into place. The jackass looked me up and down, from head to toe, like a street walker he was considering hiring. "Don't like to be called Darlin'?" He laughed like the dirty old man he was. "Right. You must be a Yankee." He smiled at me with tobacco-stained teeth.

"Actually, I'm from Fairhope, and grew up in Baldwin County, if that matters." I said. How could this pig confuse his unattractiveness and my professionalism for northern heritage? Breathe Katie, just breathe, I told myself, wanting to be anywhere but dealing with his guy.

"You must be one of those women who has trouble with her sexuality," said Polyester Shorts with a sneer and a wink.

I dug my French manicured nails into my palms just to keep my mouth shut. "Is there something I can do for you?" I tried again in my sweetest kiss-my-ass-you-fruit-loop voice. And he proceeded to tell me what the real problem was, which turned out to be a bad spark plug in a new lawn mower. Good grief. All this over a damn spark plug for his lawn mower. I authorized the trade for a new one and left the dirty old man standing there needing a complete physical and emotional makeover. The crazy thing about being a Human Resource Manager in a big-box retail store was that you got involved in strange things like this when no other managers were around.

After taking care of Mr. Spark Plug, I went back continued on my way to my safe haven, my office. My dad told me years ago that Human Resources would be a great job if it weren't for the employees. Yeah, and retail would be a great job if it wasn't for the customers. He told me this after he had worked in Management for twenty years, a good part of that time in Human Resources. At the time when he gave me his sage advice, I was still fresh meat, with only two years in the HR business. I thought he was just bitter, and I told myself that times were different now. I was wide-eyed and ready to fix all the issues my associates could bring me. I could make a difference in people's lives. I was living the dream. Now that I was seventeen years into this career, with no other discernible skills to fall back on and therefore not a lot of other career choices, I agreed whole-heartedly. Customers suck, employees suck, and don't even get me started on the people who worked in corporate offices.

My office was a twelve-by-twelve box with no ceiling, no windows and cement walls. It looked more like a jail cell than an office, but I'm repeatedly told by corporate in Atlanta, I'm lucky to work here because we have fun. Most days we do; unfortunately, today was not one of the fun days.

Before my butt hit the chair in the office, I noticed the headline on the front page of the *Mobile Press Register*. Cunningham shot down in own backyard. The article went on to recap the sordid tale of Cunningham's abuse of the boys at the church and recounted his release. It summarized the public outcry because of his release and the resulting investigation into the leak to the newspaper of information not approved for release ...

I read through the article quickly. It said that there are currently no leads yet on who shot Cunningham, but the Baldwin County Task Force was "confident that they will find the killer." They were working on the leads and thought that it would be resolved very shortly. They didn't believe that anyone else was in danger from whoever killed Mr. Cunningham and that they would work diligently to bring the killer to justice.

"The fact is that no matter what anyone may think about Mr. Cunningham, the main concern is that he was never convicted of any crime. And last time I checked, this was still the United States of America and he was innocent until proven guilty. Secondly, this is Alabama in 2006, not the Wild West in 1906. Regardless of what you think about what he may or may not have done, it is against the law to shoot people down in their own back yards." *The Mobile Press Register* had quoted a statement by Task Force member Wes Harmon of the Baldwin County Sheriff's Department. The rest of the article continued to summarize the public reaction to the release of Mr. Cunningham, including many members of the legal community.

I noticed that I wasn't breathing and took a breath. For the first time since pulling the trigger, I was scared. Not scared that I'd done the wrong thing. Not scared that he may have been innocent, as Mr. Harmon had said to the newspapers. I was scared that I might be caught. I had relived every minute of the event in my mind. Replayed each step, tried to remember if I forgot anything that might cause my capture.

I reread the article and statements by others involved. Jennifer Kollman said, "He deserved what he got. If the court system can't take care of this guy, somebody needed too. I hope they never find out who killed this sick man. I wish I would have done it myself, killed him myself. Whoever took care of this human infection is a hero. A true American Hero." There were many other quotes by the kid's family members who confirmed that this was the general feeling within the community.

Larry's brother, Tim, the church minister said, "God has his own way and his own time. I loved my brother but he had a sickness. I don't believe in killing but I apologize to everyone for all the destruction he caused to other people's lives. I'll pray for his soul and I'll also be praying for the families in my church." There was a picture of Tim standing in front of his brother's house. Tim Cunningham looked much older than he had in previous photos I had seen. I wondered if his brother's death had, in some strange way, eased the situation for him.

"Hey, Katie, did you see the midday news? That DA guy, David, is on TV talking about Cunningham. Somebody shot that guy. How cool is that!" Gayle, a nineteen-year-old ditzy blond who worked in the flooring department, stood in my open door with an inappropriate grin over a man's murder.

"Yeah, I was just reading about it," I said, finding my voice. I'm not quite sure I sounded like myself. I felt like I was in a tunnel, and nothing moved at normal speed. I grabbed the phone and called George, my friend, co-worker, and an assistant manager. "Hey, do me a favor and cover me for a minute. I need to run get a Joe Muggs. You want one?" I asked.

"God, yes! Hey, did you see somebody shot that Cunningham loser? Isn't it great!" said George.

"Sure is. I'll be back in about ten minutes. You got the store? Thanks." I was looking for my office keys to lock my door and noticed my hands were shaking "Shit," I said and shook both hands at the wrist like I was drying them off.

When I got to Joe Muggs, Ashley was behind the counter again. She knew I was a Sugar Daddy latte girl. I waved and she started brewing. I pulled up a chair and opened up the paper. As I continued to read the article, I felt a little better about everything.

From the article I learned that Larry Cunningham was shot with a rifle, a .270 or .308. The Task Force reported that his body was found Tuesday afternoon. According to his brother, he hadn't shown up at the church service on Sunday or at work on Monday. Though his brother, the minister, was not worried at that time, he assumed the controversy had finally gotten to Larry, and he was hiding at home instead of being stared at or whispered about by everyone he came in contact with. Because his body had lain in the weather for five days, much of the evidence had washed away with the rain on Saturday night, including any prints or tracks that might have helped. .

No leads, little evidence, a victim that nobody was sad was gone. The article was clear; everybody was thinking that he got what he deserved. One less bad guy running loose on the streets was no big heartache to anyone, even his family. My Sugar Daddy latte tasted much better. It appeared that things had worked well and the police didn't seem to have any leads thus far. Maybe I would be okay, at least for now.

I bought George an overpriced cup of coffee and headed back across the parking lot to my own drama.

CHAPTER 23

—————————— ▼ ——————————

The week since finding the body of Larry Cunningham had been horrible for Wes. The public had gone totally insane. The killing was being celebrated as if a local high school team had just won the state championship. Every bar at the beach was full of people talking about the "hero" who had taken responsibility for justice after the police had screwed up the situation. Whoever killed the bum was the man of the hour. The district attorney was reported to have said or beers with a couple of attorney friends that he hoped the murder was ever found, that he would "give the guy a key to the jail cell myself if the police ever got their heads out of their collective asses and found him."

Every news station reported that the shooter was the answer to a botched investigation. The damn shooter had become a local hero. Wes had been working nonstop on the Cunningham case since he had left the crime scene. The police were putting in a ton of extra hours, but Wes seemed to be the only one who cared about finding the murder.

It was not a good situation. How could he get any possible witnesses to talk to him when nobody believed that the shooter did anything wrong? Locals had actually been on the news saying that they'd like to know who shot Cunningham so they could organize a parade for the guy. One of the mothers, Jamie, said that she would gladly cook the guy dinner anytime he wanted stop by. Even the mayor said, off the record, that he would make the guy an honorary city key holder.

If the damn shooter ran for office today, he would win. It was this madness that kept Wes going back to Cunningham house. The day after the body was found was fairly normal for members of the Task Force. They did their parts, got the paperwork together, and an autopsy was completed quickly because there weren't any other bodies at the county morgue. Wes had spoken with all the mothers once he left Jennifer's house. He had interviewed Tim Cunningham, he had talked to the neighbors, but he had nothing, absolutely nothing to lead him in any direction. Everywhere he turned, there were dead ends. By day two, when the press got the information out there and the celebration that Cunningham had been shot down like a dog began, Wes came to a very important conclusion. He had to be the one to find something because nobody was going to help him. Even the other guys on the Task Force were uninterested in finding the shooter.

Several times he asked other members of the Task Force to help with interviews or tracking down a lead. They all said they would get to it, but nobody called back or even bothered to show up at the Task Force office for the scheduled morning meetings. By noon on the third day, his own Task Force members were not returning his calls.

Wes walked through Larry's back yard and into the woods where the shooter had sat in the tree stand. Wes stood for a minute at the bottom of the wooden ladder with the broken step looking up at the seat, thinking what had he missed. He had been back up the tree stand several times. This time he kept walking straight back from the stand away from Cunningham's back yard. This route took him over Polecat Creek to a red clay road. He was sure that the shooter must have parked a vehicle back there to ease away without anybody seeing him after the killing was done. The bushes weren't so thick that the murderer wouldn't have been able to walk through, but thick enough that you could not see anything on the road.

Wes felt something here on this patch of road. Over the years, he had learned to trust his gut more than his head. The Task Force was pretty sure that they were looking for a seasoned hunter, someone who knew his way around the woods. Wes started at the south end of the road, and walked all down the right side of the road, looking for anything strange or out of place. When he got all the way to Highway 55, he turned around and walked all the way back down the left side of the red clay road. Just fifteen yards from where he came through the woods and started to look, he stopped. He saw something partially submerged in the ditch on the side of the road, under muddy water and clay.

Watching his balance, he carefully made his way down the three-foot drop without slipping on the slick red clay and sliding down on his butt. He reached over the dirty red mud and pulled the object out of the water. It was a Styrofoam coffee cup. Wes wiped off the white cup with his finger and read the name on the side of the cup. He recognized the name and the logo of the coffee house instantly.

"Joe Muggs," he read aloud. There was only one Joe Muggs in Baldwin County. And that was in Daphne, fifteen miles away from this dirt road. Who drove fifteen miles to get a cup of coffee? He had been in Joe Muggs, everybody had, but it would be out of the way if you lived in this part of the county. If you were a local farmer and working this pecan orchard, Joe Muggs was probably not your favorite location for coffee. Wes had only been in there when he was shopping in the area or getting a gift certificate for his middle daughter who loved books. It was generally not a destination point by itself.

Joe Muggs was a chain of stores that rented space in national chain book stores. The coffee at Joe Muggs was not the average cup of coffee; it was expensive designer coffee, like Starbucks. They had thirty different flavors. Basically overpriced, fancy pants coffee if you asked Wes. Not what your average farmer would be drinking in the morning while he plowed the fields.

Wes smiled to himself, pulling a plastic bag from his back pocket and placing the cup into the plastic evidence bag. He turned the bag over and over in his hands. Strange that this would be here; it was truly out of place. These were the things that he liked to find. He was trained to look. Not only for what you expect to see, look for what you didn't expect to see. It was like those puzzles with a picture hidden in a picture. You had to look for what didn't belong, and sometimes it took several trips before your eyes found what doesn't belong.

Wes carried the cup back to his car. He sat for a minute, looking first at the cup, then at the front of the house. He turned the key to the car and slowly backed down the driveway wondering where this new piece of information might take him.

CHAPTER 24

▼

After one week, the Cunningham Task Force fell apart. The lack of evidence in the killing of Larry Cunningham wasn't the biggest problem. It was lack of interest that was the biggest issue with the Task Force. They had met one more time during the first week after all the reports were submitted. The meeting, headed by Wes, had turned into a Meet and Greet instead of a business meeting. Wes couldn't get anyone interested in organizing the investigation.

"Listen, Wes," said Jimmy Spence from the State Troopers office. "The guy is dead and we got nothing. Yes, we think it was a hunter, but hell man, we got what, three or four thousand licensed hunters in the area."

"That doesn't even count the number of unlicensed hunters, you know, just your good old boys that have .270 rifles" said a Robertsdale city cop that Wes didn't know. "There could be another thousand or two of those walking around."

"Point is," Jimmy started again. "Nobody cares who killed Cunningham. If we did find the guy, it would be a cold day in July that we could find a jury who would be impartial. This shooter is a hero."

"Be political suicide, that trial would," said the representative from the DA's office. "Can you imagine if the shooter is one of those angry mothers? Can't you just see that on the six o'clock news? Put the lady on the stand and drill her about killing Larry the Pervert. Then Ms. Mother of the Year comes back and says 'I had to kill him, he was going to rape by baby again, and those incompetents in the police department wouldn't help us.' Yep, that one comes to trial in Baldwin County and I'm moving to Georgia."

"Enough," Wes said. "Just because we hate the victim and love the criminal doesn't mean that they get off scot-free. It doesn't work that way."

Wes got a lot of blank stares and a couple grunts, but nobody, not even Wes, believed what he had just said.

"Okay, guys let's get back on track here. I visited the crime scene again today and found a coffee cup, Joe Muggs, on the road behind the Cunningham place." Wes ran through what he found and that he had an idea that the cup must have belonged to the shooter. He had checked with the property owner who said that they hadn't been back there for several months, since the pecan farm was harvested. He was positive that they hadn't been back there with any coffee of any kind, but couldn't guarantee that it wasn't from a couple of kids parking or drinking. However, if some teenagers had been back there parking, chances were Wes would have found beer cans and not a coffee cup. They say that it has happened before when the kids were parking and drinking beer but never coffee.

Wes also shared with the group that he had a very far-out theory about who was drinking from the cup and who may also be the shooter. The room was completely silent as he made this plea to try to get his team members interested again.

"That's real interesting, Wes. Let us know when you have something solid," said Jimmy Spence. He got up and left the room, taking Stevie, the representative from Silverhill, with him.

Two other Task Force members seeing which way the wind was blowing on this followed them out, "We'll look forward to hearing how it goes Wes. Good luck." And they were gone.

The last two members of the Task Force sat in the corner, waiting for a response from Wes, drinking their coffee and looking straight at him. Wes was dumbfounded; he didn't know what to say. He looked down at the paperwork in front of him, pushed the sheets of the forensic report on the Joe Muggs coffee cup into the folder and sat down heavily in his chair at the head of the table. The last two members of the team looked at each other with raised brows and slowly left the room. Wes was all alone.

Two hours later, Wes sat in his office with the Cunningham file spread out in front of him when the Sheriff Jackson walked up to his desk. "Wes, you got a minute?"

"Sure, what's up?" Wes asked, feeling dejected and helpless. He had been working on this case for two weeks now, he had been chewed out by the parents from the church, he had been subjected to speculation that he had screwed up the Cunningham case, and now his own Task Force members ignored him and refused to help.

"I hear that you have a theory on the Cunningham murder," said the sheriff. "Let me hear it."

"I found a coffee cup at the crime scene, a Joe Muggs coffee cup. It had a partial print on the bottom of the cup, and I was able to get a fairly good match. I believe that a local lady named Katie Race is the killer. She's a foster parent here in Baldwin County and her prints are on file with the state police. I believe that she was drinking the coffee when she got out of the car on the red clay road behind Cunningham's house, or the cup fell out of her vehicle when she went to kill Mr. Cunningham," said Wes with very little excitement.

"What's the motive?" asked the sheriff.

"I don't know. She was a member of the grand jury that indicted Mr. Cunningham. She was present at the proceeding when Cunningham was let go," he added, seeming even less sure of himself.

"That's it? You've got a female who's not related to this guy in any way. You've got no motive for why this lady would decide to kill this bastard. Has she ever been in trouble with any law enforcement agency in the past? I can answer that one myself with a no, because foster parents are put through very close inspection before they're certified. You got nothing but a coffee cup with a 'fairly good match' on the print."

"Well, I was able to find out that she's a hunter, has been for years. Actually belongs to a hunting club. She is a foster parent, so she loves kids and has taken in three very hard cases, twice teenage girls with children of their own." Wes understood he was on shaky ground.

Jackson paused for a long minute. "I heard what happened today with the Task Force. Jimmy told me he was there, and it was pretty brutal. I'm sorry for that. You do a great job and don't really deserve to be treated with that little respect. But here's the deal: you want to go after a foster parent just because she happens to like the outdoors and foo-foo coffee? Nobody wants this killer to be found. Everybody wanted this guy dead. Nobody is sorry that his ass was lying face down in his own back yard. His own brother, a preacher, isn't sorry the guy is gone. Haven't you noticed that you're the only person working this case? Don't you wonder why nobody else cares? Wes, nobody cares because we are all happy the bastard is dead!

"We're very unpopular right now. All of us in law enforcement in this part of the world are very unpopular right now over this." Sheriff Jackson put his hands in his pockets and looked at the ceiling. He drew in a long breath, held it for thirty seconds and let it out slowly, still staring at the ceiling. "Wes, I know you're a good man. You've worked real hard to get Larry Cunningham in jail and then it got all crazy. I know that Jennifer and Jamie and the rest of those ladies hold you responsible for messing up the Cunningham thing, and I know that you didn't mess it up.

"Wes, I'm going to give you some advice. If you ever say I gave you this advice, I'm going to call you a liar to your face." Sheriff Jackson looked at Wes and knew what he needed to do. "We've been friends for a long time. Hell, I think I've gotten drunk with you after both of your divorces."

"All three. You've gotten drunk with me after all three of my divorces," Wes said very quietly, more to himself than to the sheriff. "And I got another one coming, so save your money."

The sheriff laughed "Damn it, I forgot about that stripper. Man, she was a nice piece … I'll buy the first round on this divorce, too. You just let me know where and when. But you need to let this Cunningham case go. Just let it go. We can't win on this one. We got so many other cases that will help get us where we need to be as a department."

"You mean get you reelected as sheriff?" mumbled Wes.

"Yeah, that too," admitted the sheriff. "Let's just let this one go, son." And he walked out, leaving Wes looking after him.

*   *   *   *

In the Kollman household, Jacob and Jennifer sat at the kitchen table. Jacob was doing homework and Jennifer was writing checks to pay the bills.

"Mom?" said Jacob

"Yes, honey?" Jennifer answered

"I've been talking to the guys. And we think it's time to go back to our church. You know the Loxley Lutheran Church." Jacob's young eyes look at his mom, pleading.

"You think you guys would like that? I mean, with everything that happened?" she asked. She stopped what she was doing, holding the power bill in one hand and the checkbook in the other.

"We think it was wrong for the jerk to have chased us away from our church. He's gone now, anyway. Yes, we think going back would be a good idea." And with that simple logic, Jacob went back to his homework.

*   *   *   *

Jamie and her two boys had been through a lot of changes after Larry was killed. Jamie was investigated and questioned repeatedly by the press. It seemed that they were very concerned about her comment that she was "going to kill him" that day in the courtroom. Wes had questioned her several times but she had a solid alibi for the days under question and she did not own a rifle.

Jamie had turned to her ex-husband during the disaster and he had responded with sympathy and compassion for this boys and his ex-wife. They had spent a great deal of time together talking with attorneys and the DA's office. He had stayed by her side until the questioning stopped and the police seemed to move on in a different direction.

When she no longer felt like a suspect, she had thanked him by cooking him dinner. One dinner had turned into several and he had shared with her that his relationship with Sondra was over. The boys were delighted to have their father back in their lives and worked hard to push both mom and dad into spending time together. Jamie and her husband seemed to see each other in a different light and had started what could only be called 'dating'.

CHAPTER 25

▼

"Katie, where you going? Are you busy right now? I need to speak with you when you get a chance." All three questions were fired from a machine gun mouth by Linda, who thought she was my number-one associate and my new best friend. Linda had a son who just graduated and needed a job. which explained why she wanted to be my new best friend. I had agreed to interview Linda's son, more as a favor than for any real job prospect. I was living to regret that favor every day. Not only was Linda's son unemployable, he was also a lazy idiot who believed that the world owed him a job because he was eighteen years old and a high school graduate.

Linda was no prize herself, and I had no idea why I felt compelled to do her a favor and talk with the kid. A couple of weeks back, before her son needed a job, she had asked me on the sales floor, in front of several customers if I was gaining weight.

"Dang, girlfriend, you keep eating like you been and your butt's going to be as big as mine," she said at a maximum volume, loud enough not to require the PA system. Linda weighs over two hundred twenty pounds herself and was five feet tall. I weighed one seventeen and was five foot three. Pointing out these facts would have been great fun, but I would probably get fired. I must also add that, at two hundred twenty pounds, she attempted to wear the same sizes and styles that I did, and *that* was the travesty, not the difference in weight.

"Give me a bit, Linda. I need to run an errand," I said walking faster toward the door.

Out the door, across the parking lot, and into Joe Muggs I went. "Aah, sanctuary." I felt like the Hunchback of Notre Dame. My sanctuary was a in good cup of over sugared coffee and not in a church's bell tower.

It took a minute because there was a new guy at the counter, and he didn't know me by sight. He did, however, see the desperate look of a coffee junkie in my eyes and moved quickly once I said, "Sugar Daddy latte, please."

I looked to my right to see what magazines were on the shelf to read, and I felt movement to my left. Thinking it is just another customer, I got out of the way.

I looked back to my left to make sure that I am out of the way.

"I'll get her coffee, and I'll take a cup of real coffee … black, please," said a voice behind me.

I turned to see a tall, handsome guy who looked vaguely familiar, and I searched my memory for who he might be. "Thanks," I said "Do I know you?" My day was getting better: a cute guy, who looked good in a pair of jeans, buying me a cup of coffee.

"No, but I know you," he said with a sweet little smile, so friendly.

"Katie Race," I said, holding out my hand for him to shake.

"Wes Harmon," he responded, taking my hand but not shaking it, just holding it. "Baldwin County Sheriff's Department Task Force," he added and continued to hold my hand a little too long.

"Oh shit," I thought. My hand instantly began to sweat and he looked down as he released it.

"Nice to meet you," I managed to say. "Thanks for the coffee." I picked up my latte and headed for the door with a fake smile. Not wanting to run, I slowed my pace. As I got into the parking lot, I noted that he had followed me out of the building.

"Excuse me, um, Katie?" I heard from a few yards back. "Have you got a minute?" he said.

"Yes, sir?" My heart was beating a mile a minute. I was thinking that I might throw up. "What can I do for you?" I recovered and sounded okay again. "I didn't really think a nice-looking cop would just buy me a cup of coffee for no reason."

"I was just wondering. You were on the grand jury that indicted Larry Cunningham, right?" Wes asked.

"Larry Cunningham? You mean the pervert that got shot? Sure was. That was a long time ago. I saw the whole shooting thing on the news," I answered. "How did you remember that?"

"Any feelings about his being shot?" Wes leaned on a car that might have been his.

"Same feelings everybody has I guess." I looked him right in the eyes, "Kind of glad the guy isn't around to hurt any more kids."

"You wouldn't know anything about who shot him, would you?" asked Wes, with a thoughtful expression.

"Not a clue," I said. I took a big gulp of Sugar Daddy and burned the crap out of my tongue. "Damn, that's hot," I said, not meaning to say anything.

"Funny thing. We found a Joe Muggs coffee cup at the crime scene," he said.

My smile instantly disappeared. "It's good stuff, popular coffee, that's for sure." I couldn't breathe; my heart had stopped, I was sure.

"Yes, it is." He smiled "Well, it's good to see you again. I'm sure we'll run into each other sometime." He turned and walked away. I noticed that his car was unmarked and away from the others in the parking lot. It looked like he'd been watching who was going in and out of the Joe Muggs store.

I stood there, dumbfounded. What was that all about? That was it? "Wouldn't know anything about who shot him would you?" That's it? That's all? Oh God, what does he know?

Wes got into his car. He drove over to me and rolled down his window. "Hey, Katie, I forgot that I have something for you." He handed me a magazine, *Alabama Outdoors*. "I thought you might like the article on page sixty-seven. It's something that you, as a concerned hunter, might feel strongly about and you might just want to do something about it. You know, being that you're such a concerned citizen and such a good shot with a rifle." Wes gave me a little boy finger wiggle wave and drove out of the parking lot.

I stood with my mouth hanging open and watched him leave.

To keep from looking stranger than I already did, I started walking again toward my car, carrying the magazine. When I got to my office, with my coffee in hand, I sat down, still confused. What did he mean, "a concerned hunter" and "a concerned citizen?" I turned to page sixty-seven. Stuck there between page sixty six and sixty seven was a newspaper article from the *Pensacola New Journal*. The headline read, "City council member walks on sexual abuse charges."

I quickly scanned the article about an elected public official, indicted on twenty-four counts of child abuse, who had been released on a technicality.

I sat back in my chair and took another long drink of my Sugar Daddy latte.

"I've never hunted in Florida before," I said to myself as I smiled.

The world is a dangerous place to live—not because of the people who are evil but because of the people who don't do anything about it.—Albert Einstein.

THE END

978-0-595-68969-
0-595-68969-8

Printed in the United States
90711LV00004BA/22/A